IT WAS AT THAT POINT THAT THE SCREAMS STARTED.

Someone tried to hold Emma back, but she ran up after Arthur, then wished she had not, for what she saw in Guy's room was the most fearful sight that she had ever seen in her life.

He was at his desk, slumped sideways in his chair, his head hanging at a strange angle, with a great gash from ear to ear in his throat from which blood had gushed all over his chest and was still oozing in a bright crimson stream. Roger stood still behind him. There was blood on his hands and in his right hand was an open, bloodstained razor.

EXPERIMENT
WITH
DEATH

E. X. FERRARS

BANTAM BOOKS
TORONTO · NEW YORK · LONDON · SYDNEY

This low-priced Bantam Book
has been completely reset in a type face
designed for easy reading, and was printed
from new plates. It contains the complete
text of the original hard-cover edition.
NOT ONE WORD HAS BEEN OMITTED.

EXPERIMENT WITH DEATH
A Bantam Book / published by arrangement with
Doubleday and Company, Inc.

PRINTING HISTORY
Doubleday edition published May 1981
A Selection of Walter J. Black Detective
Book Club
Bantam edition / May 1982

Bantam Books are published by Bantam Books. Inc. Its trademark, consisting of the words ''Bantam Books'' and the por-
trayal of a rooster, is Registered in U.S. Patent and Trademark
Office and in other countries. Marca Registrada. Bantam
Books, Inc., 666 Fifth Avenue, New York, New York 10103.

PRINTED IN THE UNITED STATES OF AMERICA

0 9 8 7 6 5 4 3 2 1

EXPERIMENT
WITH
DEATH

CHAPTER 1

At a few minutes before half past three on a drizzly afternoon in early November, Mrs. Fallow, whose function in the King's Weltham Institute of Pomology it was to oversee the cleaners and various other domestic matters, carried the tea urn into the common room to which the members of the scientific staff could come for a cup of tea, if they felt so inclined. Helped by Dawn, a seventeen-year-old girl whose surname nobody knew, she set out cups and saucers, tea, milk and biscuits on the central table.

The room had probably once been the morning room in the Victorian mansion which, with many additions and alterations, had been converted into the Institute. The room was high, with a ceiling of ornate plaster moulding, which dated it, cream walls grown dingy with time and an elaborately carved mahogany mantelpiece surrounding a fireplace which had been blocked out with a sheet of plaster board with an electric fire in the middle of it.

Mrs. Fallow switched on the fire, though the room was not cold, for when the mansion had been converted central heating had been installed and the men and women who worked there were far more comfortable than the family and servants of the wealthy banker who had built the house had ever been.

Besides the central table on which Mrs. Fallow had planted the tea urn there were several small tables and a number of plastic chairs. There were three tall windows in one wall which overlooked the apple orchards that surrounded the building, the

1

leafless trees looking black and shiny today in the light, steady rain.

Leaving the room, Mrs. Fallow and Dawn crossed the main hall and turned left towards the passage that led, among other places such as storerooms and the darkroom, to the room where they would shortly be serving tea to the technical staff. It was a far more cheerful room than the other, having a table tennis table in it and a dart board. As she turned into the passage, however, Mrs. Fallow was accosted by Mr. Hawse, the porter, who emerged from his small, glassed-in office just inside the stately entrance to the building and, looking at his watch, said, "Three-thirty. Tea, eh?"

He was a very conscientious, punctual man who allowed himself exactly a quarter of an hour for his tea. He was fifty-seven, tall, heavily built and bald. He had once been a lorry driver but had had to abandon this after a heart attack. Work as a porter at King's Weltham suited him very well.

"I was listening to the long-term forecast last night," he said as he joined Mrs. Fallow. "Not that you can ever go by what they say, it's all nonsense, but they said it's going to be a bad winter."

"All winters are bad," Mrs. Fallow said. "I can't remember one that wasn't."

She and Mr. Hawse paused in the hall while Dawn ran on down the passage to the technicians' common room. The hall was square and lofty and looked as if it ought to have been decorated with the stuffed heads of lions and tigers, but if these had ever been there they had been removed by the banker's descendants when they were driven out of their home by succeeding sets of death duties. There was a tiled floor of intricate design and a wide staircase with heavily carved banisters, opposite the head of which, on a half landing, was the door to the office of the director of the Institute, Dr. Guy Lampard. More stairs went up to right and left of the half landing, and on the right of

2

Mr. Hawse's cubicle another passage led away to a region of laboratories and the office of the secretary, Ernest Nixey.

"I don't mind the cold myself," Mr. Hawse said. "I prefer it seasonable. Mild winters aren't healthy."

Dr. Emma Ritchie, emerging just then from the passage that led to her laboratory, overheard this remark and reflected that this was a superstition to which the British are strangely prone. Many of them go in fear of warmth and comfort. Sometimes they go so far as to believe that these will make them ill. If the wind howls and the curtains hanging over closed but ill-fitting windows flutter uneasily, letting in an icy chill, it is thought that this good fresh air will protect them from influenza, bronchitis and other associated ailments.

In his home, however, Mr. Hawse was glad of the heating that Emma Ritchie had had installed when she bought a house some years ago in the village of King's Weltham, had it converted into three flats and let the basement to Mr. and Mrs. Hawse. The rent that they paid was only nominal, but part of the arrangement with Emma had been that Mrs. Hawse should clean her ground-floor flat for her, while Mr. Hawse looked after the garden. It was his to do what he liked with. All that concerned Emma was that she should not have to cope with it herself, and what he liked to do with it was to grow long, straight rows of vegetables, interspersed in the summer with a few rows of the less interesting kind of annual, bunches of which he would bring to her with generosity and pride.

She would have passed him with a nod on her way to the common room if he had not spoken to her.

"Hallo, Miss Ritchie. I was going to look in on you this evening. I've some nice sprouts I'll bring up to you."

He was much addicted to brussels sprouts, not Emma's favourite vegetable, but she answered, "That's very good of you, Arthur. Just what I was wanting."

"There hasn't been any frost yet," he said, "but you don't

believe that story that you shouldn't eat sprouts till they've had the frost on them, do you? All nonsense. Better without, you'll see."

In the seven years that Emma had known Mr. Hawse, she had found it difficult to discover anything that he did believe in. He was a profoundly sceptical man and, working as he did among scientists, he wanted it clearly understood that nothing that emerged in their work was ever likely to shake his belief in his own odd collection of prejudices. Emma enjoyed excellent relations with him, yet he never called her Dr. Ritchie, almost as if he doubted that she had any right to the title, since she was not a member of the medical profession. In fact, she had a D.S. from London University.

She went on into the common room, which was still empty, poured out a cup of tea, helped herself to a biscuit and sat down at one of the small tables. She was a tall, slender woman of thirty-eight, whose once black hair had already turned steely grey. She wore it long, parted in the middle, looped low over her ears and rolled up in a coil at the back of her head. But in contrast to this early sign of age, her cheeks were a fresh pink and there were very few lines on her slightly sharp-featured face with its large, slatey blue eyes, pointed chin and firm lips. She was thought by some people, among those whom she did not intimidate, to be a beautiful woman.

But she intimidated a great many, to her own bewilderment, for she thought of herself as on the whole a humble and diffident person and did not realize that diffidence can create the appearance of impenetrable armour. She dressed for comfort rather than style and today was wearing a dark red jersey dress and a grey cardigan which sagged badly at the pockets because of the way she had of thrusting her fists deep into them. This was a nervous habit. If she did not imprison her hands in her pockets they had a way of fluttering about, sketching expansive gestures that looked eager and emphatic, yet which did not seem to mean anything and by which she herself was extremely irritated. She wanted, in the conflict that she tried to wage with that diffidence of hers, to appear relaxed and composed, and that was how she seemed to Ernest Nixey when, a minute or two after her, he came into the room.

The secretary of the Institute did not often come to tea there. Usually a tray was taken to his office, which was next to Emma's laboratory, by his secretary, Mollie Atkinson, but at the moment she was away, ill with bronchitis. He was a small man of fifty, with stooping shoulders and large hands and feet which gave him the look of having been intended as a much larger man, but somehow to have got shrunk by life. He had a long face and large, sad, brown eyes. The little that was left of his hair was dark brown. All his suits were dark brown too and exactly the same, and in some mysterious way had all reached the same state of shabbiness at the same time, so that it was easy to suppose that he had only one. This, indeed, might even have been the case, for his wife was in a private mental home, a fact that could very well explain both his sadness and his apparent penury.

He came to Emma's table, carrying his teacup, and said, "Mind if I join you?"

She smiled at him and he sat down.

"I don't seem to have seen you around recently," he said. "What have you been doing?"

"Writing," she answered. "Trying to write a paper. I hate it. I've never been any good at expressing my ideas."

"I'm sure you do it very well," he said. "You're just too self-critical. But it's no good my asking you about it. I shouldn't understand a word."

"Don't you sometimes get a bit bored with us all, all wrapped up in our own subjects?" she asked.

"You sometimes make me feel completely brainless." He had been trained as an accountant and was shrewd and intelligent and in any matter that related to finance could have made most

5

of his scientific colleagues appear like ignorant children, but he always made a point of asserting his own deep ignorance of what he made out to be far more important matters than any that he understood. "You know, you're the one person here I can talk to freely without feeling a complete fool."

"Perhaps you don't take me really seriously, because I'm a woman," she suggested.

"Oh, I take you very seriously indeed. My guess is that you're the most distinguished person here."

She looked amused. "Guy always excepted, I hope."

"Ah well, Guy . . ." He shrugged. "But tell me, is it true that he's done nothing really significant since he took over the running of this place?"

She was cautious. She did not want to be led into heedless discussion of her colleagues, let alone the director.

"He's stimulated a lot of other people," she said. "I'd call that significant."

"Yes, and after all we can't all do everything. I admire him enormously, as I'm sure you know—and I mean his human side as well as his intellect."

There were a good many people who did not consider that Guy Lampard had a human side, so Emma found something refreshing in Ernest's admiration of it.

He went on, "All the same, when it comes to appointments, he can do some odd things."

"Has something been settled then?" she asked.

There had been a number of rumours circulating recently about who was to fill the place of Clive Bushell, one of the senior members of the staff who had just reached the age of sixty-five and was about to retire, and she knew of at least one person who was sure of being chosen and who would be very angry indeed if he was not. But Guy Lampard, though he often confided in Emma, whom he had known for years, had told her nothing of what he intended in the matter.

Ernest Nixey gave a nervous look round the room. A number of people had drifted into it and were sitting about with their tea and biscuits, gossiping about the iniquities of the research council that controlled the affairs of King's Weltham and did not allow them as much money as they thought they needed for their research, or about the peculiarities of certain members of the staff who did not happen to be in the room at the moment, or about cricket in Australia, which they had watched on television the evening before. One or two of them were talking about their work. No one was paying any attention to Emma and Ernest except Roger Challoner, deputy director of the Institute, who had just come into the room and who gave them an interested look, as if he might be thinking of joining them, but who then turned away to talk to Clive Bushell, who would be leaving them all for good in another fortnight.

A party was to be given for him and a presentation made and Emma had been given the task of enquiring discreetly from Mrs. Bushell what she and her husband would like. Roger Challoner was in charge of the money that had been collected for the present and he and Emma had been into the town of Crandwich the day before to choose the coffee service that the Bushells had said they would value. He was a tall man of forty-eight, lean, rather pale, with rough, thick grey hair, dark eyes and a narrow, nervous face that generally had a look of hesitant kindliness on it.

Ernest drank some tea and said, "There I go, talking too much. It's you, you know. I never do it with any of the others. But one has to talk to someone. And being alone at home, the pressure mounts up. But actually I don't know a thing. Guy plays his cards very close to his chest."

"How are things with your wife?" Emma asked. "Is she any better?"

He lifted a hand in a little gesture of helplessness. "She has her good days and I start hoping, then the bad days come back. I go to see her every day, you know. I think it helps her even when she hardly knows me. The people at the home are very good to her. Wonderful, really. Such patience. That's a great consolation."

"I'm sure it must be."

"Still, at the moment I do wish Guy hadn't decided—" He checked himself, as if he had nearly said something that he knew he should not. "The fact is, I'm afraid there may be certain difficulties ahead of us."

"I overheard Arthur saying that the long-range weather forecast is for a bad winter," Emma said, deliberately flippant, because she wanted to avoid being told things that it might be awkward to know.

"If it were only the weather . . ." Ernest finished his tea, then abruptly set his cup down, turning in his chair with a faintly guilty air as the door opened and Guy Lampard came into the room.

He was a short man in his early fifties with a thick body, but curiously wiry arms and legs, which had the appearance of being able to propel him about at a velocity unsuitable to someone with his paunch and his plump, soft-looking neck and face. He had smooth, bulgy cheeks, a small, full-lipped mouth, a fleshy nose and small grey eyes which could change in their expression, from one second to the next, from the utmost friendliness to a malicious kind of intelligence, or to a totally unrevealing blankness. He could always charm when it suited him to do so. His hair was still brown, but thin, and he kept it sleekly brushed back from his formidable forehead. He was wearing a heavy knitted grey pullover, loudly checked trousers and down-at-heel suede shoes.

He was followed into the room by his secretary, Maureen Kirby, a golden-haired girl of twenty-five who was several inches taller than her employer and amply built, with a glowing pink face, a bland smile for everyone and big blue eyes. At a first glance she looked as if she would be full of warmth and friendship for anyone who asked for it. But in fact she was a reticent girl and the gaze of the big blue eyes was oddly evasive, as if she were afraid of being trapped into some relationship that she did not understand. It tended to make people feel sorry for her without quite knowing why. She was wearing a tight white sweater and a full skirt of brightly patterned velvet which did nothing to reduce her size. In her work she was extremely competent but otherwise, according to Guy Lampard, was so stupid that it was really refreshing to have her around.

She poured out a cup of tea for him, which he refused, as she must have known that he would, since he disliked afternoon tea on the grounds that it interfered with his pleasure in the whisky that he would drink at five o'clock. There had been some signs of uneasiness since he had come into the room, as it was something that he very rarely did, and generally, if he arrived there, it was for some purpose that might turn out to be disturbing.

But there were no signs of this today as he stood in front of the glowing bars of the electric fire with his hands locked behind him and his heavy body rocking slightly backwards and forwards on his heels.

"I believe we're giving you a party here next week, Clive," he said to Clive Bushell, "and then you'll be leaving us. Too bad. Why should a man have to retire simply because he's sixty-five when his mind is as active as ever? And why can't he draw his pension at fifty-five if that's all he's fit for? I'd go next year myself if it weren't for that bloody pension. One ought to have a chance to go while one can still make something of what's left of one's life."

Emma knew that this was completely untrue. Not only was Guy Lampard a man who would hold tight to his position until he was forced out of it, but he came of a family of merchant bankers and had a considerable private income. His pension, when it came, would not mean a great deal to him.

"As a matter of fact, I'm quite looking forward to retiring," Clive Bushell said. "I think I told you, we've got the cottage we wanted in Cornwall and I'm going to try my hand at a bit of painting. I haven't any talent, but I think I'll enjoy it. And of course Martha's Cornish, and she's always wanted to go back there."

"But first you're going to go off round the world, aren't you?" Guy Lampard said. "Mexico, Fiji, New Zealand and so on, didn't you say? You don't know how I envy you. I could do with six months myself out of this bloody climate."

"Yes, we're certainly looking forward to it," Clive Bushell said with a smile. "We can't really afford it, but we're going to do it. If we don't do it now, we never will."

"That's the right spirit," Guy Lampard said. "But we'll miss you here. The place won't seem the same without you. However, I've some good news about your replacement. I've at last heard from the Board of Governors that they've accepted my recommendation and it's settled at last. Sam Partlett's coming here."

There was silence in the room.

Emma thought, "So that's why he came here this afternoon. He wanted to drop this bombshell. He wanted to watch the effect of it."

Guy Lampard certainly looked as if he were enjoying himself. His small eyes shone with an excited gleam of malice.

"A difficult man, Sam, of course," he said. "He takes some understanding. But half the things people say about him aren't true. Just a bit of tolerance is all he needs to get him back onto his feet. He needs that, I admit. He needs a bit of help. But it'll be worth our while to give it to him, because he's got a remarkable mind. Given a chance, he'll bring us a lot of credit."

A chair scraped as Bill Carver stood up abruptly. He was one of the younger members of the staff, who had been at King's Weltham only three years, but he had persuaded himself, Emma knew, that when Clive Bushell retired he would step into his place, with a rise in salary as well as status. With a wife and three young children, Bill could certainly have done with it, and to make matters worse for him at this moment, he had allowed other people to know that he was taking the promotion for granted.

His cheeks burned with anger and humiliation. He was a thickset man of thirty-two, of medium height, with a quantity of fair hair that he wore rather long, bold green eyes and a tight mouth that twisted all too readily into sourness.

He did not look at anyone but walked straight out of the room, letting the door slam shut behind him.

Guy Lampard did not appear to notice it.

"Well, I thought you'd all be interested to know what's going to happen," he said. "I don't know when Sam will get here. Quite soon, I expect. He's been doing nothing since he got back from America. He can move into Clive's lab at once when he's cleared it out. God, Clive, how I wish I were starting out on a trip like yours. I'm sure it was your wife's idea. You'd never have thought of anything so enterprising on your own. Give her my regards."

He smiled around the room and went out.

Maureen gave a deep sigh, as if she were glad that the scene was over, and poured herself out a second cup of tea.

Emma stood up.

"This is what you meant by difficulties ahead," she said, looking down at Ernest Nixey as he sat, looking even more shrunken than usual, crouched over his empty teacup.

He nodded. "And of course I oughtn't to have said anything about it, but now it's out I don't suppose it matters. Not that I know anything against Partlett, but one hears rumours. But I know Guy has a very high opinion of him, and he wouldn't be wrong about his ability."

"Only about his character, you think."

"I tell you, I don't know. It's chiefly young Bill's disappointment I'm worried about. I thought he had a very good chance of Clive's job. I may even have inadvertently encouraged him to think he had, which of course I'd no right to do. One shouldn't meddle. But he isn't going to take the situation well and he won't help to make things easy for Partlett, and that sort of thing can do a surprising amount to upset the atmosphere of a place. There are enough undercurrents already. There are bound to be, I suppose, in any place where a lot of people work too close together in a little place like King's Weltham and haven't any other resources. I don't know what I'd do myself without my chess club. You're the only person who doesn't seem to get involved. Sometimes I wonder if you even know half the things that are going on."

Emma thought that this was very likely the case. She usually assumed that other people liked one another fairly well, as long as they were not openly rude to one another, and she seldom troubled herself to scrape under the surface of their apparent relationships.

"I don't suppose I do," she said, and making her way to the door, crossed the hall, nodded to Arthur Hawse, who was back in his glass box after his short break for tea, and went on down the passage to her laboratory.

It was at the end of the passage. Going along it, she passed the office of Ernest's secretary, which led into his, and the laboratories of Clive Bushell and Bill Carver. The laboratories of the other people who worked in the building were on upper floors, or in some of the extensions that had been built onto the mansion.

She kept her laboratory neat, except for a jumble of notes and books on her desk. The long window, which had replaced the two small sash windows which had once been the only lighting in the room, overlooked a mass of greenhouses, their glass roofs at present shining with the drizzle. There were two sinks in the room, a fume cupboard at one end of it, an electric furnace that was used for reducing organic matter to mineral constituents, and the usual collection of Bunsen burners, balances, microscopes, bottles of alcohol, a razor for section cutting, petri dishes and such things.

The walls were painted a pale grey. Emma had hung one picture there, a Monet print of some irises. In the seven years that she had worked there it was the only sign of her personality that she had allowed to appear and it was a long time since she had looked at it last. She was not a person who paid much attention to her surroundings.

Sitting down at her desk, she put on the glasses that she needed for close work and gazed with a look of dissatisfaction at the last page she had written. The three years of work that she had done on the influence of carbon dioxide concentrations on the survival of apples in storage seemed very easy and stimulating compared with the labour of writing a paper on the subject. But Guy Lampard had kept telling her recently that it was time that she got something written, that it would be a bad thing if she turned into one of the people who were incapable of committing themselves in print because just conceivably they might have made some error that they had not detected, and at last she had forced herself to start turning her jumble of notes into an orderly statement that could be published in the *Journal of Pomology*.

But the trouble was that basically the work bored her. Besides that, she had certain personal problems on her mind that kept coming between her and the page in front of her, which was nearly covered with her small, neat handwriting. Looking up from it after a little, she stared vacantly through her glasses, which reduced the distance to a blur, at the big window, streaked with rain, at the spread of greenhouses and at some tall, leafless trees beyond them, and let her thoughts wander. She was sitting there in a dream when the door opened and Guy Lampard came in.

He perched on one of the stools in the room.

"All right, go on," he said. "Say what you think."

She took off her glasses and his plump face came into focus.

"I did think you were unnecessarily cruel to Bill, springing the thing on him like that," she said. "You did it on purpose, didn't you?"

"He had it coming to him," he said. "He's been practically telling people he was going to step into Clive's shoes and with no justification whatever. Poor old Clive, thank God he's going at last. He's been a dead loss for the last dozen years. But I've never said a word to Bill to give him the idea he'd a chance of the job. He's just got a too bloody good opinion of himself. Actually he's got no imagination or originality, he's just got a reasonably competent pair of hands, which are quite useful so long as someone else is telling him what to do with them. That's all. I've no use for him."

"Or he for you."

"And you think that ought to worry me."

"I think one should always worry at provoking unnecessary dislike."

Emma and Guy Lampard had known each other for a great many years and could speak freely to one another. She had been one of his Ph.D. students at London University before he had gone as professor of biochemistry to the University of East Sussex, then he had appointed her to a lectureship in his department there, and when he left it to become director at King's Weltham, he had persuaded her to follow him. Her attitude to him had always been ambivalent. She regretted a number of his peculiarities and was not afraid to tell him so, yet under the surface she had a great deal of affection for him.

"Well, what do you think about bringing Sam Partlett here?" he asked. "Don't you think it's a good move?"

"I don't know anything about him," she answered.

"Oh, come, surely you've heard he's impossible, that he's always got across everyone he's worked with and never stayed anywhere for more than a year or two. And recently he's been drifting around America, never staying anywhere long enough to get tenure, and finally got fed up with things and came home. And there he is now without a job of any sort, utterly wasted."

"Then what's so clever about bringing him here? Won't he go on getting across everyone?"

"I don't think so. I can handle him."

"Those might be famous last words."

He shook his head. "No, really. We're very old friends. I understand him. And he's brilliant, you know, no one's ever questioned that, and we can do with a little of that here. It's too easy to get into a comfortable rut in a place like this and stay there. That's one of the reasons I didn't even think of trying to get Clive's job for Bill. I don't hold with internal appointments."

"What makes Partlett get across everyone? What's wrong with him?" she asked.

He gave her a wary look, as if to make sure that she really did not know the answer. Then he shrugged his shoulders.

"Envy, I expect," he said vaguely, and she felt sure that her question had been avoided. "There's a lot of that in academic circles, as you know. And he's a bit irresponsible perhaps, and he doesn't suffer fools gladly. But I've always found him very easy to get on with myself. We speak the same language. And I think I can give him the kind of conditions he needs. And that reminds me, there's something I want to ask you."

"I thought there might be," Emma said. "I didn't think this call was purely social. What d'you want me to do for him?"

His short, heavy body wriggled slightly, as if in embarrassment. He often put on an air of being unsure of himself when he was with Emma, which she knew was quite unreal.

"Don't hesitate to say no if you'd sooner not do it," he said.

"Tell me what it is."

"Well, the Bushells will be moving out of that top-floor flat of yours in two or three weeks' time, won't they? I wondered if you'd feel like letting it to Sam and his wife until they've found a house for themselves."

He was referring to the flat above Emma's in the house that she had bought and converted when she first came to King's Weltham and which the Bushells had rented straight away and remained in ever since. They had been perfect tenants, considerate, helpful, quiet, and she doubted, from what she had heard, if the Partletts would compare very favourably with them. But she always felt reluctant to refuse Guy anything he asked of her. It was not often that he did so.

"Partlett's married, is he?" she said, temporizing.

"Yes, to a very charming little woman."

The phrase meant, for certain, that Guy had never had any interest in her, perhaps had hardly noticed her existence.

"The place is only part furnished, you know," Emma said. "Most of the stuff in it belongs to the Bushells and they'll be moving it out. I only put some furniture into it in the first place so that I could keep control and get rid of any tenants I didn't like. You can't turn people out if you've let a place unfurnished. But of course I've never wanted to turn the Bushells out. I'm only too sorry they're leaving."

"But is there enough furniture for the Partletts to camp out up there for a time, if they haven't any stuff of their own? For all I know, they've got plenty which they left in store when they went off to America."

"I should think there's just about enough. I suppose I could lend them a few things, linen and so on, if they need them."

"That's splendid. Then I can tell Sam they can have the

place for a time, can I? That'll help a lot. Sam can just get to work without worrying about finding a place to live first, and so on. That'll get him started off in the right way. I'm immensely grateful, Emma." He slid off the stool, looked over her shoulder at the few pages of writing that she had achieved, remarked, "You're not getting on very fast, are you?" and with his rapid, springy strides left the room.

Realizing that, without really intending it, she had accepted the Partletts as tenants, Emma put on her glasses again, switched on the light on her desk, because with the steadily falling rain the afternoon was growing dark early, put her elbows on the desk and her head in her hands and gazed steadily and unfruitfully at a new, blank sheet of paper.

Suddenly something clicked in her mind. She realized what had set up the block that had prevented her writing. It was a failure to interpret a quite simple piece of evidence. She began to work fast, filling a couple of pages before she again began to have doubts of herself and to become aware that she was very tired. She looked out the window. It was dusk outside and the roofs of the greenhouses had become mere geometrical shapes dimly outlined in the twilight. Laying down her ballpoint, she stood up, put on the tweed coat that was hanging from a peg on the door, tied a scarf over her hair, let herself out of the laboratory and walked along the corridor to the entrance.

Her car, an aged Renault, was in the car park. As she walked towards it, she saw Guy ahead of her, without hat or coat in spite of the rain, striding towards his home, a pleasant house that had been built for the director of the Institute near to the main building. Guy lived there with Dorothy, an ancient housekeeper who long ago had been his nurse and who now, except that she still did a little cooking for him, was looked after by him as much as he by her. A woman from the village came in to clean the house while Dorothy enjoyed a well-paid and sheltered old age. There was a great deal of loyalty in Guy's nature, which sometimes showed itself to people whom he did not like nearly as well as he liked the aged Dorothy.

Emma drove towards the village. It was built more or less in a square with a green and a duck pond in the middle, a very old church with a squat, square tower, a prefabricated village hall, two pubs, a densely packed collection of cottages, mostly of stone, and several surprisingly good shops. Emma's house, one of the few Edwardian buildings in the village, was covered with white roughcast, with green shutters at the windows which were mere decorations and could not actually be closed. It stood a little way back from the main road into Crandwich. When she first came to live in King's Weltham there had been nothing but open fields between it and the town, but recently they had become linked by a chain of bungalows, which were gradually spreading and would no doubt soon engulf the village, turning it simply into a suburb of Crandwich. For the present, however, it still had an identity of its own. Emma drove her car into her garage, closed the door and locked it and made her way in what was now nearly darkness to her front door.

It opened into a small vestibule with two doors facing her. One opened onto a staircase that led up to the Bushells' flat, the other into her own. The flat in the basement, occupied by Arthur Hawse and his wife, had an entrance of its own at the side of the house, which had once been its back door. Emma put her key into her lock and opened the door.

There was a light on in her sitting room. Its door was open and she could see the glow of the electric fire and a pair of long legs extended across the hearthrug in front of it. As she went into the room Roger Challoner got up from the chair in which he had been sprawling and she went into his arms.

Before she put up her face to his, she said, "I was hoping for this. I'm glad you waited."

CHAPTER 2

"I'd nearly given you up," Roger Challoner said. "I thought perhaps you were having dinner with Guy."

"I just didn't realize how late it was." Emma untied her scarf and smoothed her hair in front of a mirror that hung over the fireplace. "He did come to see me, but not to ask me to dinner. He wanted something else and I think I've been a fool to agree. Let's have a drink."

Roger went to the table on which a tray of drinks stood and poured out sherry for them both while Emma took off her coat and returned to the narrow hall to hang it up on one of the row of pegs there.

Coming back into the sitting room, she dropped onto a sofa facing the fire and put her feet up.

The room was a long one with windows at each end, the farther end of it used as a dining room, with a round table, some chairs and a sideboard in it, all undistinguished Victorian that Emma had inherited from her parents, and the near end a comfortable sitting room with deep armchairs, a coffee table, a television, a gramophone, some bookcases filled with a mixture of scientific works and paperback thrillers, and only one good piece of furniture, a Georgian tallboy that also had come from Emma's childhood home. Its drawers were filled with papers, records, sewing materials, photographs and anything else for which she could find no other home. The curtains were of a soft shade of dark blue and Roger, who had a key to the flat and came and went as he chose, had already drawn them.

He brought her her sherry and stood on the hearthrug, looking down at her.

"I'm very tired," she said, pushing a cushion behind her head. "I suppose it's because I'm worried. As I said, I think I've been a fool."

"What did Guy want?" he asked.

He seemed very tall, standing over her, with a look of kindly concern on his face. That concern, which he showed very readily when he was discussing the troubles of others, always moved Emma, although she knew by now that behind it there could be cool detachment, almost amounting to indifference, if he felt that the troubles in question were not being handled with a reasonable amount of intelligence. She had found out long ago that he was not quite the humane and tolerant person that he appeared, a fact that at times made him seem even more difficult to deal with than Guy, whose prejudices were all out in the open.

"He asked me to let the Bushells' flat to the Partletts," she said. "And I found I'd agreed before I'd even thought about it. Roger, what *is* the trouble with the Partletts that people talk about? What's wrong with them? I tried to get it out of Guy, but he just dodged the question."

"I don't know much about Partlett myself," Roger answered. "I've met him once or twice and he seemed quite inoffensive. Colourless, even. And very reserved. But there must be more to him than that or Guy wouldn't have gone on taking an interest in him all this time. He was one of Guy's Ph.D. students, as I suppose you know, a bit before your time, and they must have kept more or less in touch ever since. I gather he's quite harmless when he's sober."

"Oh, is *that* the trouble?" she said. "I'm letting the flat to a drunk. That doesn't sound too encouraging."

"That's only what I've heard. It may not be true. He didn't show any signs of it when I met him."

"And Mrs. Partlett?"

"I don't know anything about her. I shouldn't worry too much. You don't have to see much of them if you don't want to."

"It's just that we've been such a wonderfully well-adjusted household all this time. I'm going to miss the Bushells, though Guy's glad to be getting rid of Clive."

"Naturally. He's part of the old staff, like me, whom Guy had to take over with the furniture when he came here."

"He doesn't want to get rid of you."

"No?"

"No, of course not."

"I wouldn't be too sure." He emptied his glass, reached out for hers and crossed the room to refill them. Returning, he sat down in one of the chairs by the fire, and watching her face intently as he spoke, he said, "I've been toying again with the idea of that job in Adelaide."

She felt a chill run through her, as she always did when this subject came up. "Seriously, Roger?"

"Well, don't you think perhaps it's time I did?" he said.

"I don't really see why."

"It's a dead end for me here. Guy's never going to do much about getting me any more money for research, particularly now that Partlett's coming here. And I heard again this morning from the people in Adelaide. I'd have all kinds of facilities that I'll never get here. They still seem to be interested, but that won't go on forever if I don't make up my mind."

Emma nodded. Roger had heard for the first time from a distinguished research institute in Adelaide about six months ago and the offer carried far better working conditions and a higher salary than he would ever achieve at King's Weltham.

"And the fact is, you want to go," she said sombrely. "Partlett's coming here has just tipped the scale."

"It depends on you," he said. "You know that."

"We've been over and over that. Is there anything new to be said about it?"

"I won't go if you're really against coming too."

"A gun at my head?"

"You know that isn't how I mean it. You've always known I'd never go without you."

"But I haven't faced how much you want to go. If you really do. Are you sure of that?"

He smiled uncertainly. "This evening I am. Perhaps tomorrow I shan't be."

"That's the old story. That's how it's been from the beginning. But as long as one feels one can still change one's mind, one doesn't really face a situation. And indecision undermines one in all kinds of ways. You can reach a point when you're so worn out by it that you've a sort of horror of thinking about the problem at all. I've quite stopped thinking about it for some time."

"And you don't want to start again."

"There are so many things involved. For one thing, we'd have to get married, shouldn't we? They're used to us here as we are, but I don't suppose you could turn up at a new job in Adelaide with me just loosely attached."

"Have you so much against getting married? Really, it's a very small objection, isn't it? It isn't the significant thing."

There, of course, he was right. Marriage would make only a minor change in their relationship. And the fact that they were remarkably happy as they were did not mean that they might not be even happier if they slid into the traditional behaviour of married people and lived openly together. Vaguely Emma had always supposed that that was what they would do in the end. They had been lovers for two years, a fact so well known to everyone at King's Weltham that it had long ago ceased to be of interest, even as gossip. Really, all that kept them from getting married was a kind of inertia, a habit of going on as they had begun. There was something very private about it that appealed to them both. Emma had been married for a time when she was young but had only been thankful when she had found herself released, and to go once more in front of a registrar, recite a formula and sign a paper would mean very little to either of them. On the other hand, if, practically speaking, it should be desirable, there was not much against it.

"No, I suppose it isn't," she said. "But what should I do with myself if I'd no job of any sort? I'm a bit old to think of having children, and even if we tried that, perhaps it wouldn't happen. Can you see me dwindling into being just an academic wife?"

"With your qualifications you could get a job out there, and even if there wasn't one going at first, you could certainly get a room to work in."

"It's a bit of a gamble, isn't it?"

"I know it is. All right, we'll forget about it."

"Or keep our options open just a bit longer."

"I thought it was you who couldn't stand indecision."

"Well, it's both of us, isn't it? When you come down to it."

"I'll only add something," he said, "then we can stop talking about it. I think one of your reasons for not wanting to leave King's Weltham is your dependence on Guy. As long as you've had him behind you, as you've had from the beginning, you've never had to stand quite on your own feet, scientifically. I think you could do it if you wanted to, but you're just scared. Now what are we going to eat this evening? Is there any food in the house, or shall we go out?"

"There's plenty in the house. But you can't expect me to let you say a thing like that and then suddenly stop talking about it—"

The doorbell rang.

It was Arthur Hawse with the brussels sprouts he had promised Emma. They were as fine as he had told her, not loose and shaggy, but each one looking like a tightly curled, dainty, miniature cabbage. She only wished that she enjoyed their flavour more. She asked him in, but he said that the missus was just dishing up and that he'd be in trouble if he lingered.

He did linger on the doormat for a little, however, saying that he was thinking of buying a greenhouse, if she wouldn't object to his erecting it in the garden, next to the shed that he used as a garage. She assured him that she would have no objection at all. By the time he left Emma had lost the impulse to start an argument with Roger about her relationship with Guy. She went straight to the kitchen to prepare a meal, cooking the sprouts, sautéeing some potatoes left over from the day before and grilling chops. She was an adequate if not imaginative cook. She and Roger followed the chops with cheese and fruit, then had coffee by the fire. They did not return to the subject of the job in Adelaide.

He stayed the night instead of returning to his lodgings in the village, but afterwards Emma wished that he had not. There had been an odd element of desperation in their lovemaking, as if both had realized that if either of them made a mistake now it was not impossible that they could lose one another. It was hardly a conscious thing, yet afterwards they held one another for a long time, as if they were cautiously drawing back together from a precipice.

Lying awake later after Roger had fallen asleep, Emma wondered what had really made her feel the dread that had invaded her. A dread of responsibility perhaps. Roger had put his future in her hands. Or at least he wanted to make her think that he had. Knowing as she did the firmness that lay behind his gently considerate manner, she knew it was possible that his own mind was clearly made up already and that it was her own future that was in the balance.

He drove off to work earlier than she did the next morning. It was one of Mrs. Hawse's mornings for coming in to clean. She was not quite as friendly a person as her husband and disapproved of Emma's relationship with Roger and perhaps, if she had not liked her flat as much as she did, would have wanted to move away. She showed her disapproval by a cold-eyed refusal to notice that Emma had had a visitor. But she was a conscientious woman and, according to her agreement with Emma, kept the flat immaculate. She was devoted to the Bushells and was very grieved at their leaving. She said that she hoped Emma's next tenants would be as nice, though one could hardly expect that. Emma did not tell her that the flat was already promised to the Partletts.

She did not see either of the Bushells for some days, or much of Roger either. Both he and she had various engagements for the next few evenings, then he had to go to a scientific meeting in Birmingham, at which he was giving a paper. Her own paper progressed by fits and starts. Sometimes she found it easier, then suddenly more difficult than she had at first. Then one evening, as she was arriving home, it happened that Martha Bushell arrived home at the same time and Emma invited her in for a drink.

Following her in, Martha gave a cheerful little titter and said, "I've had one already, but I don't suppose it matters if I have another."

Martha could become cheerful on one small glass of sherry and a second made her feel that she was really being a devil. She was a short, firmly corseted woman of sixty, with curly brown hair that she had discreetly tinted, a pink and white face that had only recently begun to show her age and large blue eyes behind the latest fashion in spectacles.

As Emma poured out sherry for them both, Martha went on, "I've been to my bridge this afternoon and we always end up with a round of drinks. I do so enjoy it all. I'm going to miss it terribly when we leave. There are just the four of us and we've been meeting in each other's houses for such years now. I really don't know where I'd have been without my bridge. It's different for someone like you, of course. You're creative. I used not to understand that scientists are creative. I thought they just went ahead and did experiments and proved things. But Clive says they're just as imaginative as artists. All the same, I should have thought it might do you good to have some distraction now and then, like a nice game of bridge. Tell me, Emma, is it true what Clive told me—I think Guy told him—that you're letting our flat to the Partletts?"

"I haven't heard anything from them yet," Emma said, "but Guy wants me to offer it to them."

"Oh, my goodness, if you can, get out of it!" Martha Bushell exclaimed. "They're perfectly *terrible* people!"

"You know them well, do you?" Emma asked.

She herself would have found it difficult to write anyone off as perfectly terrible unless she was sure that they had committed murder, rape, blackmail or some serious slander. In the world in which she lived slander was the most probable of these crimes, but also the one most likely to be casually taken for granted.

"Not exactly *well*," Martha said. "I met him once at one of those international congresses I went to with Clive and I thought at first what a pleasant little man he was. It surprised me, because I'd already heard things about him, you see, and I thought how unfair everyone had been to him. And then one evening, all of a sudden—it seemed to happen from one minute to the next—he started insulting everyone and I realized that actually he was fearfully drunk. I don't know how many drinks he'd had before Clive and I and the rest of our party joined him, but he seemed to do his best to pick a quarrel with Clive. Well, you know how impossible it is to do that. He's just never learnt how not to turn the other cheek. But as soon as we could we found an excuse for getting away."

"So what you're telling me is, Partlett's an alcoholic," Emma said.

Martha gave an uncertain frown. "What I've heard about

him, though I've no firsthand knowledge of it, is that when he gets drunk he gets violent. Smashes things and so on. But I really don't know if that's true. The evening I met him he wasn't violent or anything like that, he was just abominably rude."

"What's Mrs. Partlett like?" Emma asked.

"I don't know anything about her," Martha answered. "She hadn't come to that congress with him. I've been told they quarrel a great deal, in fact that she's left him more than once, but always comes back to him again, heaven knows why. I can't imagine leaving my husband without a very good reason, but once I'd done it, that would be that. But then when someone's been as lucky in their marriage as I have, I don't suppose one understands much about that sort of thing. And anyway, it may not be true. But one thing I can tell you about him which I believe really is true—I've heard it from several people—he once tried to kill himself."

It gave Emma an uncomfortable sense of chill.

"You said *tried*," she said. "Why didn't it come off?"

"I don't know. I don't even know how he went about it. I mean, poison, the gas oven, cutting his wrists or what. It may even not have been a genuine attempt. You know what I mean. Some people put on a show of trying to commit suicide, just to draw attention to themselves. I should think he might easily have done something like that, particularly if he was drunk."

Emma gave an uneasy laugh. "Well, I hope I don't see blood starting to drip through one of my ceilings one day. If he tries it on again, I hope it isn't in one of the messy ways. I wonder what it is that's made Guy so attached to him."

But as she said it, she thought that she knew the answer. Guy Lampard had always been attracted by the misfits in life. Whatever success came his way, he would never overcome the feeling that he was one of them himself. As a boy, Emma knew from stories he had told her, he had been bullied at school and had not had much love in his home. He had kicked his way up to his present position by sheer intelligence, determination and a readiness to stab a rival in the back, if it would serve his turn. He could be extraordinarily unscrupulous if the mood took him. But to the badly maladjusted he was nearly always generous. It was to the contented, the well liked, the people who in their private lives were very successful, like the Bushells, that he was most unkind.

Martha finished her drink and stood up.

"Perhaps you shouldn't listen to me," she said. "After all, it's all just gossip. But they do say suicides will try the same thing over and over again if they don't succeed at first, don't they? Oh dear, I shouldn't be talking like this. I'm only upsetting you. And actually you needn't see anything much of those Partletts, if you don't like them. We've seen as much of each other as we have because we became such friends straight away. We're going to miss you terribly, Emma. Remember you've promised to come and stay with us in Cornwall as soon as we're settled."

She left Emma feeling that she would like to telephone Guy immediately to tell him that she had changed her mind about letting the Bushells' flat to the Partletts.

However, she knew that if he put any pressure on her to stick to her half promise she would give in to him. She knew that Roger had been right when he said that she had never outgrown some degree of dependence on Guy, and one of the things that this had done to her was that she had never learnt how to assert herself when he leant on her heavily, as he occasionally did. Wandering about the room after Martha had left, Emma dug her fists deep into the pockets of her cardigan and did her best to assure herself that it had been very good-natured of Guy to find her new tenants for her empty flat so quickly and that all would be well.

It was about a fortnight later that she first met the Partletts. The Bushells had been given their farewell party, for which the wives of the members of the staff had provided cold meats, salads, trifles and mince pies, while Guy had furnished a lavish supply of drink. The presentation had been made, as well as a few speeches, and then the following day the Bushells had had their furniture moved out of their flat into storage and had started on the first hop of their journey round the world. Martha had given Mrs. Hawse a generous parting present and when the Bushells had left she went into the flat and cleared out cupboards, removed remnants of straw and paper scattered about by the removal men, and polished what furniture was left. When the Partletts came to look the place over, it was somewhat bare but spotless. If the beds had been made and there had been food in the refrigerator, they could have moved in on the spot.

Emma had had no picture in her mind of what they would be like, yet as soon as she saw them she knew that they were not what she had been expecting. They were both small people, of about the same age and the same height. Perhaps Mrs. Partlett was an inch or two the taller, as certainly she was the heavier. Sam Partlett was lean and wiry, with a hollow chest and a smoker's hoarse cough. His hair was sandy and cut very short, showing the shape of his skull. He had grey eyes under bushy sandy eyebrows and hard, rather expressionless features. He was wearing a checked jacket, baggy trousers, a grey and white striped shirt which was not very clean, and a slightly frayed blue tie. His wife had thick curly dark hair which she wore down to her shoulders, big, rather staring dark eyes, high-coloured cheeks and a wide, soft-looking mouth. Her body was soft-looking too, bulging a little inside a too tight green corduroy trouser suit, over which she wore a short jacket of speckled fur fabric. They both looked shy, somehow oddly young for what were obviously their ages, and ill at ease.

Their shyness disarmed Emma. Leading them into her own flat, she gave them coffee and chatted amiably to them for a little while before she took them upstairs to inspect the flat above.

Mrs. Partlett, whose name she soon discovered was Judith, did most of the talking for the two of them. Sam Partlett stayed a little way behind her as she went from room to room, inspected cupboards, murmured appreciatively at the convenience of the kitchen and the charm of the bathroom, said what a beautiful view there was from the living-room window and how kind of Emma it was to be willing to let the flat to them.

Emma said that she hoped that they had some furniture of their own to bring in, as what was there was hardly enough to live with.

"Actually we haven't really anything," Judith Partlett said, "but what's here is just fine. We sold off what we had when we went to America. It seemed the obvious thing to do, as we weren't thinking then of coming back. Not that we had much. We never think ahead very far and somehow that means one doesn't accumulate possessions. We can pick things up bit by bit after we move in."

That sounded to Emma as if the Partletts were not thinking ahead to finding themselves a house in the neighbourhood, as Guy had told her that they would, but might be meaning simply to take possession of the flat and stay there. She was not sure that she liked this. It might work out perfectly well, as it had with the Bushells, but in case it did not, she thought, she must make sure when her solicitor was drawing up the lease that she could turn them out if she wanted to.

Looking at Sam Partlett thoughtfully as he strolled along silently behind his wife, her glance was met by a smile of singular charm. It was as if he had guessed what was passing through her mind and wanted to reassure her. Or was he mocking her? Afterwards she found that she could not make up her mind about it.

The Partletts moved into the flat on the following Saturday. They came in a Volkswagen which they told her they had recently picked up secondhand. They brought a number of suitcases, some armfuls of overcoats, dressing gowns and other garments that they had not troubled to pack, a typewriter, a radio and not much else.

Going to the door to give them the keys of the flat and the garage, Emma invited them to have dinner with her that evening to save them the bother of cooking while they were settling in. Judith Partlett protested that they did not want to put her to any trouble, then accepted gratefully, on the condition that they might come in the clothes they were wearing. They had so much to unpack, she said, and besides that they wanted to go round the village shops to buy provisions for the weekend. Sam Partlett gave Emma another of his delightful smiles. There was nothing mocking about it this time, she decided, it was just unusually sweet. Perhaps Guy was right about him after all, she thought, and there was nothing wrong with him as long as he was handled in the right way. She began at that point to be on Sam Partlett's side and to think that if he had difficulties at King's Weltham she would do her best to support him.

He was very quiet that evening, drank very little and, as before, left most of the talking to his wife, who wanted to know about buses into Crandwich, the shops there, the public library, and who the best local doctors were. She had been a nurse once, she said, and was wondering, now that she was back in England, if perhaps she should try to take up the work again. She seemed to be a simple, friendly woman, uneasy because her husband said so little, but doing her best to fill any gaps in the conversation left by his silence. Roger joined them for dinner and stayed on after they had left, which they did early, saying that they were very tired.

Helping Emma and himself to brandy, he said, "Well, how are you going to get on?"

"Quite well, I should think," Emma said. "They seem remarkably harmless."

"You've only seen the surface so far," he said. "Do you know what worries me?"

"No, what?"

"Why should Guy take so much interest in someone quite so colourless? It isn't like him."

"It may have something to do with that attempted suicide I told you about." Emma had told Roger what she had heard from Martha Bushell. "After his fashion Guy's always had a lot of compassion for people who can't cope with life."

"Um. Maybe. Anyway, why did the chap try to kill himself? He doesn't look the type."

"Is there a type?"

"I suppose not. No, it was a silly thing to say."

"After all, he's been a bit of a failure, hasn't he? He's said to be so gifted, yet he's never got anywhere. If that happened to one, one might all of a sudden feel things were too much to bear."

"Just as long as he doesn't have another go at it upstairs," Roger said. "That's something you could do without."

"Put baldly like that, it sounds a bit callous," she said, "though of course I agree with you. But I believe you've taken a dislike to him. Why's that?"

"Still waters, perhaps. I don't think we saw much of the real man this evening. Or the real woman either, if it comes to that."

"I rather liked her."

"Well, you've done enough for them. You can leave them now to look after themselves." He sat down on the sofa beside her and slid an arm round her. "Let's forget them, shall we?"

Emma did not see much of the Partletts during the next few days. When Sam Partlett moved into the laboratory where Clive Bushell had worked ever since she had first come to King's Weltham, she went in and said that if there was any way in which she could help him to get settled in he should come and tell her. Standing in the middle of the room, looking oddly lost in it, the small man thanked her and said that she was very kind. Next day he looked in on her with his first request. Would she tell him, he asked, where the photographer hung out.

She told him where the darkroom was and he thanked her again, then asked her where to go in Crandwich to hire a television. She gave him the name of the shop where she had hired her own. He enquired then if she could recommend a garage. There was an excellent one, she told him, in King's Weltham, to which she took her own car to be serviced. He still lingered uncertainly, as if there were other questions which he knew that he had intended to ask but that all of a sudden he could not remember. He turned abruptly and went out.

Later that day he appeared diffidently in the common room and Emma introduced him to the people who were there. For some days after that she did not see either him or Judith. He did not come to the common room again and in the evenings, though Emma sometimes heard them walking about upstairs and knew that they were at home, they were very quiet. It was plain that they were not likely to be intrusive. Emma was pleased. It looked after all as if they were going to be excellent tenants.

Then one afternoon she had a curious conversation with Sam. He had come into her laboratory to ask her to whom he should apply for the supplies of chemicals that he needed. She told him that the man who was in charge of such things was Stanley Rankin, the head technician, and she directed Sam to Rankin's office.

He thanked her in his quiet way, then, propping himself against her desk, remarked, "You and Guy are old friends, aren't you?"

"Very old friends," she answered.

"Ever been in love with him?"

She was so startled that it took her a moment to answer. "No."

He said, "That came out a bit slowly. Was it difficult to make up your mind how to answer?"

"I was simply astonished at being asked the question," she said.

"It seems a fairly obvious thing to be curious about. But I was expecting to be told to mind my own business."

"And that's probably what you should do."

"But even now you aren't angry with me."

"How do you know how angry I am?"

He shook his head. "You're puzzled, but not angry. You've none of the signs."

"I'm slow to wrath," she said. "Anyway, the question seemed to me merely absurd. One doesn't get angry with an absurdity."

"It's interesting that you think it's absurd. I've known Guy for years, you know, longer than you have, but that's a side of him I know next to nothing about. I know there've been women, but none of them lasted. Only you. But you say you've never been in love with him. Didn't you even have an attack of hero worship for him when you were young?"

"Oh, that's different. Yes, I did, I think. He seemed to me a very great man."

"But doesn't any more?"

"May I ask the object of these questions?"

"Only that I'd like to understand him better than I do. I've been out of touch with him for a long time. But I'm an object of his charity, you know. He thinks he's done a tremendous thing for me, bringing me here, and I can't help wondering what's in it for Guy."

"Didn't you want to come here?"

He gave her a long, serious look, as if they were in the middle of a quite impersonal discussion, then he said in a low voice, "I hadn't much choice. One's got to live, or so they tell me." He moved away from her desk. "Sorry if my questions have seemed a bit mad. I just wanted your opinion. You seem to like him better than most of the people here do, but that's really just loyalty, isn't it?"

"I've a lot to be grateful to him for," Emma said, "if that's what you call loyalty."

"Ah, gratitude, that's a terrible thing, a dangerous thing. Well, thanks for failing to tell me to mind my own business. That was very good-natured."

He gave her his sudden smile and left the room.

Emma saw him again that evening. It was in the White Hart, the smaller of the two pubs in King's Weltham, a low stone building with a thatched roof and a faded sign swinging over its doorway, a quiet place down one of the narrower village streets, where they did a very good steak and chips. Emma and Roger often went there for a drink and supper after the day's work if Emma did not feel like cooking. She did not feel like cooking that evening. She had been disturbed by her talk with Sam Partlett in the afternoon and had had difficulty in getting back to work after it, and even after she had managed to do so, she had felt restless and ill at ease. Leaving their cars outside Emma's house, she and Roger set off along the dark street to the pub.

As they entered it, she heard a laugh that she recognized. It was Guy Lampard's laugh, ringing out above the murmur of talk in the bar. He was there with Sam Partlett, the two of them sitting side by side on a settle in a corner of the room with whiskies on the table in front of them.

Guy hailed Emma and Roger at once and insisted that they should join him and Sam, which was not what they really wanted to do, and Sam got swiftly to his feet, asking them what they would have to drink. There was something excitedly exuberant in his manner, quite different from anything that Emma had seen in him before. When Emma asked for sherry and Roger for beer, he tried to persuade them to drink whisky.

"We're several ahead of you," he said, "so it's only fair if

you'll try to catch up. Come on now, whisky, or even a martini—
they don't make a bad martini here, I've tried it—but for God's
sake forget about that sherry, Emma, it isn't a real drink at all."

His speech was very clipped and his eyes were bright and
there were patches of red on his normally pale cheeks. He was
pretty drunk, Emma realized, and thought with regret of the
peaceful evening that she and Roger had intended to spend
here. If Guy was drunk he did not show it, but then he never
did. He could sit drinking for a whole evening and walk out as
apparently sober as when he had started.

Emma stuck to her sherry and Roger to his beer and Sam
stood up, picking up the glasses that he and Guy had emptied.

"That's something my father taught me," he said. "Always
stand up before you pick up the glasses, don't try to do it with
your hands full. A useful piece of advice. Not that either of you
looks as if you'd ever have much use for it. I can recognize
chronic sobriety when I see it."

He walked away towards the bar, ordered the round of drinks
and brought them back to the table. When he had sat down
again beside Guy he leant across the table towards Roger.

"You didn't want to join us, did you?" he said, his voice a little louder than before, so that several people in the bar turned
their heads to look at him. "If Guy weren't the boss, you'd have
pretended not to see us. Hard luck on you. You wanted a quiet
evening with your girl, didn't you? A nice girl. I like her. You've
got good taste. She tries to tolerate me even when she thinks I'm
intolerable. But you can't turn your back on Guy, can you? It
wouldn't be politic. I'm sorry for you. I wouldn't want to in-
trude on you for anything. But Guy's one of the facts of life you
can't ignore. Good old Guy. In your place I'd spit in his eye,
but I can see you haven't got that in you. Lick his boots, that's
more your style—isn't it, Guy? Isn't that what you expect the
whole bleeding lot to do for you?"

Guy gave an indulgent smile, as if Sam's antics amused him,

but he seemed to have become aware that Sam's voice had risen and that the other voices in the bar had been lowered.

"No need to shout," he said softly.

"And why the hell not?" Sam demanded, louder than ever. He was staring steadily at Roger, as if he found something about him intensely annoying. Pointing a thumb at Roger's tankard of beer, he observed clearly, "That's horse piss you're drinking."

"Seems all right to me," Roger said.

"Listen to me," Sam said. "I say it's horse piss. I know. I've tried it. Not fit to drink and don't anyone tell me it is." His hand shot out and grabbed the handle of Roger's tankard, lifted it in the air and brought it down crashing on the table.

The handle came away in his hand and the tankard broke into fragments. Beer splashed over Roger's face and jacket.

He stood up. "Sorry, Guy, but that's enough of that," he said. "We'll be going."

"Sit down!" Sam roared. His voice seemed strangely powerful for so small a man. "What's a little beer? Can't you take a joke? Bloody dull if people can't take a joke."

Except for his shouting, there was complete silence in the bar. All the regulars, quiet men, most of them farm labourers, were watching the scene with a mixture of interest and embarrassment. Emma saw a curious smile on Guy's face. It was almost gleeful. To her surprise, she realized that he was enjoying himself.

But he said, "Pipe down, Sam. This isn't one of your Soho pubs. You've done enough."

"I have, have I? Is that what you think?"

Sam slid his hands under the edge of the table and gave a heave. It tilted, the glasses slid off it and splintered on the floor. He waved the hand that still had the broken handle of Roger's tankard in it and gave a hoot of savage pleasure. The table fell on its side, catching Emma's foot under it. She felt a sharp pain and let out a small cry.

Roger saw what had happened and heaved the table up again. Sam tried to topple it once more, but Len Carey, the innkeeper, a big man who had once been a policeman, emerged from behind the bar and took Sam by the shoulders. Sam immediately seemed to become very small in his grasp, a shrunken wisp of a man.

"I think it's time you took your friend home. Dr. Lampard," the big man said. "We can do without this kind of thing here."

"Sorry about it, Carey," Guy said. "Send me the bill for the glasses."

Len Carey nodded, as if that had been his intention in any case.

"We don't like trouble here," he said.

"Trouble!" Sam yelled. "You've seen nothing yet. Wait till I'm in the mood!"

"You won't be welcome, sir," Len Carey said stolidly and, keeping one of his great hands on Sam's shoulder, propelled him to the door.

He went without any attempt at resistance. Giving Emma and Roger a quick little grin, which was too sardonic to be one of apology, Guy followed him out.

"Now that it's peaceful, shall we have our steak and chips after all?" Roger said.

Emma agreed and as the surface of the table at which they had been sitting was wet with spilled beer and had splinters of broken glass sticking to it, they moved to another table and ordered more drinks and their supper. Conversation around them gradually became normal again.

"How's your foot?" Roger asked. "It looked as if that table came down on it hard."

"It's all right," Emma said. "It startled me, that's all."

"I'll get my car," he said, "then you needn't walk home."

"Don't bother. I'll manage. But now we know, don't we, if

38

Sam often makes scenes like that, why he gets across people? That's been puzzling me."

"But Guy enjoyed it."

"You thought so too, did you?"

Roger nodded. "He knew what was coming. I've a feeling he set it up. He was waiting for it."

"Well, if that's what he likes, he must think we're an awfully dull lot at King's Weltham. I wonder if he's seeing Sam safely home. It can't be very pleasant for his wife if he often comes in like that."

"I expect Guy's looking after him."

But, presently, when they walked home, Guy's car was not parked outside the house. If he had driven Sam back to it, he must have gone straight on to his own home.

Emma unlocked the door and she and Roger went into the flat. As they went along the passage to the living room, he put his arms round her and she stood still, leaning her head back, so that her cheek brushed against his. But before either of them could speak there was a crash over their heads. It sounded as if something had been violently overturned, perhaps a chair or a small table. Then there were rushing footsteps across the ceiling, then a shrill scream, then another. Then footsteps came pounding down the stairs from the flat above, a door banged and there was hammering on Emma's door.

Roger turned quickly to open it.

Judith Partlett hurled herself through it, slamming it behind her. Her face was streaked with blood and there was a welt on one cheek. Her mouth was puffy and one eyelid was discoloured.

"For God's sake, lock it, bolt it!" she screamed. "Don't let him in! He's dangerous!"

Then she slid to the floor in a faint.

CHAPTER 3

For a moment Emma and Roger stood listening, but there was
no sound of footsteps following Judith down the stairs. All the
same, Emma slid the bolts on the door shut, while Roger gathered Judith up in his arms and carried her into the living room.
As he laid her down on the sofa she opened her eyes, looked
round her wildly, then closed them again. But this time she
closed them deliberately to shut out something that she could
not bear to look at. She was not unconscious.

Upstairs there was a dull thud, then silence.

"It sounds as if he's passed out," Roger said. "Perhaps I'd better go up and see if he's all right."

Judith struggled up on the sofa. "No, leave him! Don't go
in!"

She was wearing a nylon nightdress and a quilted flowered
dressing gown that was only half fastened. Her body had a
soapy scent, as if she had just had a bath. She had evidently
washed her hair, too, for it was wet, hanging in dripping strands
about her shoulders.

"He'll be all right," she said. "He always is."

Emma went into the kitchen and came back with a bowl of
cold water and a cloth. Kneeling beside the sofa, she began to
bathe Judith's face.

"Does this sort of thing happen often, then?" Roger asked.

"Not often, no. Not for a long time now. I thought he'd got
over it." Judith lay back against the cushions and, becoming

aware of how her dressing gown was gaping, began to button it with fumbling fingers.

"All the same, I think I ought go up and see how things are," Roger said.

"You can't," she said. "You won't be able to get in. I left my key inside. Please, please leave him."

"I've got a spare key," Emma said. "I think Roger should go up to make sure he's all right. We won't let him come in here. You needn't be afraid."

Judith gave a heavy sigh. "I can't stop you."

"Where's the key?" Roger asked Emma.

"Top left-hand drawer in the bureau," she answered. She was still gently bathing the bruises on Judith's face. "Has he hurt you anywhere else? Ought we to get a doctor?"

"No, no, for God's sake—don't say anything to anyone!" Judith closed her eyes tightly again, then, opening them, peered into Emma's face. "I haven't apologized for bursting in on you like this. I'm sorry, I shouldn't have done it. But I get so scared when it happens, I lose my head. I'm very sorry."

Roger had left the flat. Emma could hear his footsteps going up the stairs to the flat above.

"That's all right," she said. "I don't know what else you could have done."

"He's so quiet most of the time, you know," Judith said. "He'll feel terrible about it tomorrow—if he remembers it. Sometimes he blacks out on it and won't believe it's happened. Then when he finds out it really did, he hates himself so much, I get quite frightened. Did you know he tried to kill himself once? That was why he did it. It was just self-hatred."

Emma heard Roger's footsteps overhead.

"I heard a bit about it," she said. "When did it happen?"

"Oh, years ago. Before we got married. In fact, that's how we met. I was a nurse in the hospital when they brought him in. And I thought I could help him, and I think he thought so too."

She gave an ironic smile. "I tried it for a while, about a year, and then I left him. But he came after me, he wouldn't leave me alone. He said I was his only hope. So I went back to him and tried again. But people like Sam don't really want to be helped. He wanted me for a victim, that's all. That's what I believe now."

"How did he try to kill himself?" Emma asked. "Sleeping pills and a bottle of brandy?"

"No, he tried to hang himself." Judith said it almost casually, as if this thought had been so much in her mind that it had become a commonplace. "In the lab. He was still working for his Ph.D. and Guy happened to come in and find him and cut him down in time and got the ambulance and came with him to the hospital and while Sam was there he used to come in and visit him every day. Nobody else worried about him. His parents were both dead. Not that they'd ever cared much about him. His father was in the army and Sam wasn't the sort of son he'd wanted. And he'd nobody much in the way of friends. Sometimes I think that ought to have warned me, but at the time I just thought people were callous and that Guy was wonderful."

"How did Sam feel about being rescued?" Emma asked. "I've a feeling that if I ever got to the state of wanting to take my own life I'd hate anyone who prevented it."

"Oh, he does hate Guy, of course," Judith answered. "But he loves him too, you see. It's complicated."

The hall door opened and shut and Roger came into the room.

"He's all right," he said. "Just clean passed out. I've put him on the bed and taken off his shoes. He'll be all right in the morning. He'll have a bad headache, I imagine, but that's all."

Judith sat up. "I mustn't bother you any longer, then. I'll go up to him."

Emma looked at her battered face and saw the anxiety in her staring dark eyes. She shook her head. "You'd better stay here tonight. Then we'll go upstairs together in the morning and make sure that things are really all right. I've got a spare room. I'll just make up the bed."

"But I can't put you to all that trouble."

"It's no trouble at all."

"What about some brandy now?" Roger asked. "I think we could all do with it."

Judith hesitated, as if she were wondering if at that moment she could face the thought of alcohol, then she gave a nod, but when Roger brought her the brandy she sipped it cautiously, then gave a convulsive shudder.

"I wonder if you could let me have a towel," she said. "I was washing my hair when Sam burst in on me and it's still soaking wet."

"Of course," Emma said, and went to fetch the towel.

Judith put down her glass, took the towel and rubbed her hair vigorously, then buried her face in it, looking from the way her body started to shake as if she had just burst into tears. But when she lowered the towel and handed it back to Emma, her eyes were dry.

"I'm sorry I'm so hysterical," she said. "It isn't fair to inflict it on you."

Emma had sunk down on the floor again beside the sofa. Looking up at Roger, she said, "Judith's just been telling me about how Guy once saved Sam's life when he tried to hang himself. It's made me think of something Sam said to me this afternoon. He said gratitude's a terrible, dangerous thing. Is that how he really feels about Guy, d'you think? That he's terrible and dangerous?"

"Well, we'd a feeling in the pub that Guy was egging him on to drink, hadn't we?" Roger said. "We thought Guy enjoyed the scene Sam made."

"Did he make a scene in the pub?" Judith asked.

Emma nodded.

"Was he violent?"

"More so than they're used to in the White Hart," Roger said.

"And he was with Guy?"

"Yes."

Judith lay back again on the sofa with a look of extreme weariness on her face.

"Then that explains everything. Oh, God, why did we ever come here? I didn't want to, but I thought the danger was past. Sam's been so normal for such a long time. Normal for him, at any rate. He's always been restless and sure that things would be better somewhere else, but there hasn't been any trouble like tonight for a couple of years. And the money we'd saved in America was almost gone and no one but Guy would offer Sam a job. His reputation had got around, you see, even when people didn't know the truth about him. I'm afraid I haven't told you the actual truth about that suicide of his. He'd been out with Guy the night before and they'd got very drunk. At least, Sam got very drunk. You can never tell if Guy's drunk or not, can you? He sits there, looking as sober as a judge, when Sam's getting ready to wreck the room. And Guy saw Sam home that evening to the flat he was living in in Soho with a girl and went away, and Sam did his best to kill the girl. Some people living downstairs heard her screaming and they broke in and rescued her and found she was terribly injured. So they took her to a hospital and said they'd found her in the street and that she must have been mugged. It wasn't the sort of district, you see, where people liked to get mixed up with the police. So Sam didn't get into any trouble, but next morning he went very early to the lab and tried to hang himself."

"Did you know that story when you married him?" Emma asked.

Judith shook her head. "He told it to me after the first time he'd knocked me about. He was in an agony of remorse, and of fear too—fear that I'd leave him and fear of what he might do to me if I didn't. I think there's a terrible fear at the back of his mind that one day he might commit murder. And he told me to go and begged me not to, almost in the same breath, and I felt terribly sorry for him and said of course I wasn't thinking of leaving him, but I got him to promise he'd give up drinking completely. And he did for about three days. Then he went out with Guy again and that was that."

"Did Guy know the story about the girl Sam nearly killed?" Emma asked.

"Oh yes."

"So that's why he was so good to him when he was in hospital. Sheer guilt."

"Yes, I suppose so. But people told us he'd changed very much since he'd become director here, and got older and mellowed. Otherwise I don't think I'd ever have agreed to come. Not that I could have stopped Sam, once he'd made up his mind. But Guy can't really have changed much, can he?"

"What will you do now? Stay here or go away?"

Judith thrust her fingers through her dark hair, which was drying into curly tendrils.

"I haven't started to think about that yet. I've nowhere special to go to. And the awful thing is, I love Sam most of the time. It's only sometimes I feel I can't stand things any longer and I've got to have the courage to make a new life for myself. I'd be quite glad to go back to nursing. But then I think that if I did he might try to kill himself again and perhaps that time he'd succeed."

"Has he threatened to do that?"

"Not exactly. And I know it's just a sort of blackmail, and I oughtn't to give in to it, but all the same, it's a terrifying thought. It isn't easy to ignore it."

"Of course not." Emma got to her feet. "Now I'll go and make that bed up for you. Would you like some aspirins?"

"I think I would." Judith put a hand to her bruised cheek.

"This is fairly numb now, but it'll hurt a bit presently. I'll come and help with the bed."

"No, just stay quiet. I'll only be a few minutes."

Emma made up the bed, put a hot water bottle into it and a bottle of aspirins and a glass of water on the table beside it, and saw Judith comfortably settled for the night. As comfortably, that was to say, as was possible in the circumstances. The look in Judith's dark eyes did not suggest that she was likely to sleep.

Returning to the living room, Emma picked up her brandy and sat down on the sofa.

"Perhaps I should open a home for battered wives," she said. "You never know, I might turn out to have a gift for it. Roger, if you were Judith, could you stand it?"

"I'm sure I couldn't," he answered. "But it always amazes me what some women will stand."

"The problem of battered husbands and what they could stand doesn't often arise, does it? I think I'm going to talk to Guy about it tomorrow. He seems to be at the bottom of the trouble."

"D'you think that will do any good?"

"It might. If I tell him what happened here tonight, he might go more carefully about putting temptation in Sam's way."

"Will you tell Judith what you're going to do?"

"Of course not. She'd say at once she didn't want me to do anything. She's probably regretting talking to us as much as she did. One of the awful things for people like her is that they've a horror of talking openly to anyone about what they're going through."

"Then mightn't it be dangerous to interfere?"

"It might be equally dangerous not to."

"She and Sam may sort things out together tomorrow."

"Only till next time."

He looked dubious. She saw that he had no belief that a few words with Guy would make the slightest difference to the

Partletts' problem and did not want her to deceive herself into thinking that she could do anything helpful other than listen patiently when it was wanted of her. But he did not argue with her any further.

In the morning Emma got up early and made tea and took a cup into the little bedroom where Judith had spent the night. She was out of bed already and was buttoning her quilted dressing gown. She gave a smile that looked lopsided because one cheek was swollen and murmured thanks for the tea, but she would not stay for breakfast or allow Emma or Roger to go upstairs with her.

"He'd hate it if you did," she said. "He'd be so humiliated. That's to say, if he remembers anything about it. And if he doesn't, it'd be a bit difficult to explain what you were doing there."

"But will you be all right?" Emma asked.

"Absolutely all right. There'll be a rather terrible scene of remorse, which I'd sooner you didn't see, but that's all. There's just one thing . . ." Judith hesitated. "You've been so good to me, I don't like to ask anything more, but if you wouldn't mind . . ."

"Yes?" Emma said.

"If you see him in the lab, don't say anything about last night. Just act as if it hadn't happened."

"You're sure that's what you want?"

"Quite sure."

"All right," Emma said but, as she was saying it, reflected that it was not a promise to say nothing to Guy.

Roger left for the Institute earlier than she did that morning. When presently she arrived there and went in at the main entrance, passing Arthur Hawse in his little office, said good morning to him, she thought that he looked at her curiously and seemed about to speak. It made her wonder how much he and

48

his wife had heard of what had happened the night before. They might well have heard Judith's screams and the crashing of furniture. But she did not want to have to discuss them with him. Going along the passage to her laboratory, she paused for a moment outside Sam Partlett's door, but there were no sounds from behind it. She had not really expected that there would be, though she did not know how long it would take him to recover after a bout like last night's. She rather hoped that it would take him all day; in fact, it struck her that an attack of strategic flu, which would keep him at home for several days, would be very convenient for everyone.

In her laboratory she took off her coat, then returned along the passage to the short flight of stairs that led up to Guy's office. As she went up them she was conscious of Arthur Hawse watching her with unusual concentration. It convinced her that he and his wife had heard the uproar last night and that sooner or later she would have to give them some explanation of it. However, before she did that it would be as well to decide what she thought about it herself. Did she mean to let the Partletts stay in her flat? She was still haunted by a vision of Judith's bruised face and terrified eyes and felt an angry compassion for her, at the same time thinking with dread of hearing those screams again and of knowing that at any time she might be called in to do something about them.

She knocked on Guy's door, heard his "Come in!" and went in and found him dictating letters to Maureen Kirby.

The room was a large one with a high ceiling that had strips of fluorescent light across it, a big window through which sunshine was pouring this morning, brightening the gold of Maureen's hair and falling across the big, littered desk behind which Guy Lampard sat, tilting his chair backwards and forwards.

"I'm sorry," Emma said. "I'll come back later." She turned to go.

"No, it's all right," Guy said, "we've just finished. That's all, Maureen."

Maureen stood up, looking large and splendid in her tight white sweater and swirling velvet skirt, gave Emma one of her bland, evasive smiles and swept out. Her office was at the top of the stairs that led up to the right from the half landing where Guy's was. As the door closed behind her, Guy tilted his chair backwards again and put his hands behind his head.

"I wish that girl wasn't quite so huge," he said. "She diminishes me." With his paunch, his plump cheeks, the folds in his neck that bulged above the collar of his loose sweater and his normal air of self-assurance, he did not look in the least diminished. "Come and sit down. What's on your mind? Trouble, is it? You've got that look about you. Damn it, I don't feel like trouble this morning."

Emma took the chair in which Maureen had been sitting. "But you've been expecting it, haven't you?"

He looked puzzled for a moment, then he said, "Oh, you mean about that affair in the White Hart. I'm sorry about that. I hope it didn't spoil your evening."

"I don't think you mind in the least what it did to my evening," Emma said. "You'd a lovely evening yourself, hadn't you?"

He gave a little grin. "Well, Sam's a bit of a change after everyone else here. You never know what he's going to do next. That's what I've always found so fascinating about him. He might have wanted to spend the evening discussing Whitehead, or have gone berserk, as he did. You'll like him when you get to know him better."

"It was fascinating, was it, that he should go home and beat up his wife?"

"No—he didn't do that!"

"He did."

"Last night?"

"Yes, after you'd got him drunk in the White Hart and driven him home and dumped him on his doorstep."

He gave her a hard stare. "I don't believe you. That woman's told you God knows what yarns about him and you've just swallowed them. He wasn't drunk enough for that last night."

"He was. I don't know how many drinks you'd had before we arrived, but you don't start knocking tables over in the White Hart unless you're pretty far gone."

"And I'm to blame for this for some reason, am I? Was I drunk too? We'd had just the same number of drinks."

"You know you can drink all night without it affecting you. Sam Partlett can't."

"That's his fault then, isn't it? Why are you blaming me? The things I take from you, Emma! Sometimes you make me out a kind of monster."

"Sometimes I think it's what you are, Guy," she said. "You know you were egging him on and that sooner or later that was going to lead to violence."

The little grin twitched again at his full lips. "And you don't understand the attraction of that, do you? You've never felt it."

"I don't think you've ever felt it yourself. Not real violence, not violence itself. It's vicarious violence that thrills you. You can indulge in it through Sam Partlett without its being any risk to you. And it's why you're such a danger to him. I don't suppose you actually want him to go home and beat up his wife, but you do want him to act out all the violence that's bottled up inside you."

For the first time since Emma had come into the room anxiety showed in his small grey eyes.

"Was she badly hurt?"

"Badly enough."

"Did she need a doctor?"

"She wouldn't have one."

"Good. Because once before, you know . . ." He checked himself.

"She told us about that," Emma said. "But this isn't the first time it's happened to Judith."

"And it was real, not something she'd faked up to get your interest?"

"Well, we heard her screaming, then she bolted down to us with her nose bleeding and a great bruise on her cheek and this morning she's got a terrible black eye. She spent the night in my spare room. And she seems to blame it all on the effect you have on Sam. And that's really why I came to talk to you."

"Go on," he said coldly.

"You know yourself if she's right," she said. "Is she?"

He looked away towards the window and was silent for a time, blinking his eyes against the sunlight that streamed in at it.

"Possibly she's right," he muttered. "Or partly. I'm not responsible for what Sam is."

"But couldn't you try . . . ?" Her hands came out of her pockets and she made a fluttery, indecisive gesture with them. "You could at least be careful not to encourage him to drink, couldn't you? That wouldn't cost you a great deal."

"Perhaps more than you think. You can't change a whole relationship overnight. And it's one that's been important to us both, you know, just as it is."

"But if you'd just try to help him, instead of making things worse . . ."

He turned his head to regard her once more. He was smiling again. It was not the almost malicious little grin of a few moments before, but one of affection.

"You're really very naïve, Emma," he said. "It's one of the things I love about you. You aren't aware of it, but you know so little. You can't change people like Sam, you know, not with all the good intentions in the world. So why try? If that woman had a grain of sense, she'd leave him."

Emma stood up. "So you won't try to help."

"I didn't say that."

"But it's what you mean, isn't it?"

"We'll see, we'll see. You really don't understand the temptation he is to me, do you?"

"No, I don't. And I don't want to turn the Partletts out of my flat, but I couldn't stand many more nights like last night."

"I'll promise you one thing," Guy said, "I won't walk into temptation. How about that? Does that reassure you?"

"Not very much," she said, and let herself out of the room.

Later in the morning Emma had a visit from Bill Carver. He strolled into her laboratory, saying that he hoped he was not interrupting her but looking ready to stay for a talk whether he was or not.

During the three years that he had been at King's Weltham she had never got to know him well, though from time to time he had attacks of confiding in her. What he usually told her about was how dissatisfied he was with his job, how much he disliked Guy Lampard, how badly he felt himself underrated and how unjust life was. Emma thought that he half hoped that she would repeat these things to Guy. Bill knew that her relationship to Guy was closer than that of anyone else in the Institute, and with the vanity that was characteristic of him, he took for granted, she felt, that she would take his side.

In fact, even when she was in sympathy with him, she never repeated anything that he said to Guy. She thought that Guy was often unfair to Bill out of a simple dislike which nothing that she said would affect. In fact she would only make things worse, she thought, for Guy could not stand any interference with his way of running the Institute. He would let her attack him personally, as she had that morning, but professionally even she had to accept the fact that he considered himself above criticism.

Bill Carver hitched himself onto a stool and said, "Well, how d'you like your new neighbours?"

She took off the glasses that she had been wearing while she wrote and rubbed her eyes wearily. She had slept very little the night before and was beginning to realize how tired she felt.

"They're all right," she said.

"No trouble?"

"Why should there be?"

"Oh, I was just having a chat with old Hawse a few minutes ago," Bill said. "He thought something was up last night and said he nearly went upstairs to see if he could lend a hand, then things quietened down and he thought he'd better not interfere. What d'you make of Partlett?"

"I hardly know him."

"I think he's a slimy little bastard."

"Mrs. Partlett seems all right. I rather like her."

"Hawse said he heard her screaming last night. Is that really true?"

Emma shrugged her shoulders. "I shouldn't pay too much attention to him. He's an old gossip. It may have been something on television."

Bill's smile was quizzical. "Yes, of course, television. That explains everything. But they must play it pretty loud if Hawse could hear it in the basement. Doesn't that get you down?"

"A bit," she said. "But I don't want to make a fuss about things like that right at the beginning."

"Particularly as it wasn't television, was it? Emma, my dear, you're not a good liar. What really happened?" His bold, greenish eyes searched her face.

"How should I know?" she said. "Roger and I were out for most of the evening. But that reminds me . . ." It did not remind her of anything, but she had just had a new idea which suddenly struck her as a good one. "I think life may be a bit grim for Mrs. Partlett, coming here and not knowing anybody, so I thought I'd give a small party for her to meet a few people. Say tomorrow evening, Wednesday. No—" It had just occurred to her that by next day the marks on Judith's face would not have had time to fade. "Wednesday of next week. Just wine and cheese. Could you and Irene come? I'd like Judith to meet Irene."

Emma herself had never warmed much to Irene Carver, whom she thought a dissatisfied young woman who encouraged her husband in his not very realistic ambitions. All the same, Emma thought, she and Judith might take to one another and it really would be a good thing if Judith began to meet a few of the other wives in King's Weltham.

"And I suppose you want me and Partlett to meet and be friends," Bill said sourly. "Dear peacemaking Emma. But it won't work, you know. He's got a way of letting me see he knows he's got the job I ought to have and that he enjoys it like hell, which is rather more than I can take."

"Well, it won't do you any harm to meet him away from the lab," Emma said. "But it's your wives I'm thinking of, not you. Will you come?"

"Tomorrow week? Thank you, yes, unless Irene's got something else laid on, but I don't think she has."

"That's good. About eight o'clock then."

He got off the stool. "And there was no screaming last night, and no trouble, and you've got delightful, quiet neighbours who are going to be a great acquisition to this charming little community of ours. All right, I'll go along with that, if it's what you want. But you won't fool anyone, you know, unless you can find a way of silencing Hawse."

He went out.

Emma sat looking after him. She hated the thought of the story of what had happened in her house last night going the round of the Institute, probably growing as it went and becoming even grimmer than it had been. And she was not at all sure, now that she came to think of it, if her idea of giving a party for Judith had been a good one. Perhaps she and Sam were not on speaking terms at present. Perhaps she was packing up, getting ready to leave him. Perhaps she would not be exactly grateful if she and Sam were to be invited to a party at which drinks, even a very moderate quantity of inexpensive wine, were to be served. But Sam would probably regard that wine as practically a soft drink, and Judith, if she had made peace with him, should have nothing against it. The really worrying problem at the moment was how to silence Arthur Hawse. And the sooner it was done, the better.

Emma stopped to speak to him on her way home for lunch. She did not usually go home for lunch, as all that she ever had then was a sandwich and it saved trouble to take this with her when she left home in the morning and eat it in the laboratory, making some instant coffee to go with it, rather than to drive back to the village. But today she decided to go home. Besides talking to Arthur on her way, it might be a good thing, she thought, to find out if all was reasonably well with Judith.

"Hallo, Arthur," she said, stopping at the entrance to his office. "I hope we didn't disturb you last night."

"Well, we did wonder what was up," he said, "and if maybe you wanted help, but then everything went quiet, so we didn't come up in case it would only be a nuisance. We thought if there was anything we could do, you'd come down for us. You know we're always there, ready to help in any way we can, if ever you need it."

He spoke casually, but his eyes on Emma's face were watchful.

"Yes, I know," she said, "and it's so nice to know that. You and Mrs. Hawse are always so good to me. I'm very grateful—I do hope you understand that. But luckily things last night weren't as bad as they sounded. I was scared at first when I heard Mrs. Partlett scream. I couldn't think what was happening. Then Dr. Partlett came running downstairs and asked me to come up at once and help. It seemed Mrs. Partlett had tripped on the edge of a rug and fallen and hit her head on the fender. She'd fainted and he was terribly scared—he isn't at all a practical sort of man—and he wanted me to call a doctor immediately. He didn't know one himself, as he and Mrs. Partlett haven't had any occasion to go to one since they got here. But then she came round and wouldn't hear of having a doctor. But I got her to come downstairs with me and stay the night, in case she'd hurt herself more than she realized. Luckily she seems all right this morning. All the same, I'm going to look in on her now, just to see how things are. A bump on the head can have unpleasant aftereffects."

Emma knew that she was talking too much, but once she had got started on her string of lies, she did not know how to stop.

Arthur Hawse nodded gravely. "Concussion," he said. "You're quite right, you didn't ought to take it lightly. Sometimes, they say, it's worse if you don't crack your skull than if you do. The brain swells and there's no room for it. Nasty thing. Well, you tell Mrs. Partlett if there's any way Mrs. Hawse can help, just let her know. Could you do with some nice leeks this evening?"

Emma said that they were just what she wanted and, aware that he was undeceived by her account of Judith's accident, drove home.

When she arrived she went to the telephone and dialled the Partletts' number, but the telephone went on and on ringing for so long that she began to think that the flat upstairs must be empty and that perhaps Judith had once more decided to leave Sam and had already packed up and gone. That she might simply have gone to shop in the village, where she was known, with her face in the state that it was in, seemed unlikely. Then just as

Emma was about to put the telephone down, the ringing stopped and Judith's voice said, "Yes?"

"It's Emma—I just wanted to make sure you're all right," Emma said.

"I'm fine, thank you," Judith answered in such a distant tone that Emma was taken aback.

"Can I do any shopping for you?" she asked. "Is there anything you want—milk, bread or anything?"

"No, thank you, I've got everything we need." Judith's voice was cold and remote, as if she wanted Emma to recognize that the experience of the evening before had not led to any kind of intimacy between them. "I'm sorry I troubled you last night. It was really unnecessary."

"I'm glad that's how you feel today." Emma could not prevent some irony getting into her voice. It irritated her that she had laid herself open by telephoning to a snub of this kind. She did not want fulsome gratitude, but she had expected at least some responsiveness. "By the way, if you happen to meet either of the Hawses, the version they've been told of last night is that you tripped over a rug and fell and banged your head against the fender."

"I see. Thank you."

"Not that they believe it, but it was the best I could do."

"It's very kind of you," the frigid voice said.

Emma put the telephone down abruptly and went out to the kitchen to make a sandwich.

She supposed that she had been a fool to try to make any contact today with Judith, that it was only natural for her to try to shed the burden of her considerable obligation by making out that the whole thing had been unimportant. Yet Emma was very annoyed at the sheer discourtesy of the rebuff. Her annoyance made her think that she would abandon her scheme of giving a party for Judith and that she would not go out of her way to be helpful again.

But by the time she had eaten the sandwich and drunk some coffee she had begun to feel that she was being small-minded and that perhaps in Judith's place she might have acted exactly as Judith had. Only it was difficult to put herself in Judith's place. How impossible it was to imagine, for instance, what she would do if Roger were suddenly to start knocking her about. Would she come back for more, as Judith had? Of course not. But then it was impossible to imagine kind and stable Roger ever doing such a thing. As she reflected on how fortunate she was compared with the woman upstairs, pity returned and she decided to stick to her plan of trying to help her in whatever small ways she could.

She let three days pass before she telephoned Judith again to invite her and Sam to her party. Slightly apprehensive as she did it, in case she was given another slap in the face, she was relieved when there was no chill in Judith's voice as she answered. She accepted the invitation cheerfully, said how nice of Emma it was to ask them and how pleasant it would be to meet some of the other wives. She said that so far she had not met any of them and that being so isolated was beginning to get on her nerves, but she said it without marked self-pity. Emma recognized how Judith hoped that she would think of their disastrous evening. Quite simply, it had never happened.

Thirteen people came to Emma's party. Besides Roger, the Partletts and the Carvers, she invited Ernest Nixey, Maureen Kirby, the local doctor and his wife, an elderly retired colonel and his wife and a couple who had only recently come to King's Weltham, he as a biochemist and she as an agronomist. Emma also invited Guy Lampard, but without even troubling to make up an excuse he declined, which was what she had expected. Parties of the kind that she was giving bored him and he felt it unnecessary to disguise the fact.

They rather bored Emma too, but she thought that the sooner

Judith met some people besides herself the better it would be, not only for Judith's sake, but for her own. She would feel better once responsibility for Judith's peace of mind, not to mention her safety, was spread out rather more thinly than it was at present. Buying rolls, biscuits, cheeses, pâté, olives and some wine that she knew was drinkable, if not distinguished, she set them out on the dining table at one end of the living room and went to her bedroom to change.

She had only one dress for such occasions, a black silk jersey dress with a narrow silver belt, which she had been wearing now for several years. Every time she put it on she promised herself that she would buy herself another dress next week, but when it came to the point there was always something else that she wanted to do more. The truth was that she intensely disliked buying clothes, distrusting her own judgement and fearing that she would let herself be talked into buying something that did not really suit her, although, without her being aware of it, her tall, slender figure and her fine colouring conferred distinction on quite commonplace things. She had just finished changing when she heard the first car arrive and went to the front door to admit Colonel Branksome and his wife.

Mrs. Branksome was a large, vigorous woman and about the most potent force in village activities. Emma did her best that evening to interest her and Judith in one another, with the thought in her mind that if the old woman took a liking to Judith she would draw her into the Women's Institute and perhaps the local archaeological society or the drama group, according to what Judith's abilities were, and out of the inbred life, with its jealousies and rivalries, of the Pomology Institute. But Emma's good intentions came to nothing. Mrs. Branksome happened to be particularly attached to Roger and kept as firm a hold on him as she could.

It was Ernest Nixey who settled down beside Judith, brought her things to eat and kept her glass full. Emma, standing near them, heard him telling her the sad story of his marriage. Sooner or later he always did this with any new acquaintance who showed the slightest sign of sympathy, and there was a look of shy charm about Judith this evening which was just what he would find attractive. The marks on her face had faded, her dark hair was brushed out over her shoulders, and she was wearing a pale yellow dress with a thin gold chain round her neck. A fine topaz hung from the chain. She kept toying with the pendant, as if to bring it to Ernest's notice, until at last he said, "That's a very charming necklace."

She smiled. "Isn't it?" she said. "My husband gave it to me a few days ago. He found it in that antique shop in the square in Crandwich."

Sam Partlett was talking to Bill Carver, or rather, Bill was talking with a good deal of animation to Sam, who looked rather sullenly aloof. For the first time that Emma had seen, he was wearing a suit instead of his shabby checked jacket and trousers. The suit was old-fashioned yet looked almost new, as if it had hung unused in a wardrobe for years.

"Charming," Ernest said again. "A nice little town, Crandwich, isn't it? Of course, it was incredibly good fortune for us, in our particular circumstances, that there was a private mental home of the standard of Manstead House there. There so easily might not have been anything of the kind in such a small place. But as it is I can drive in every day and sit with my wife for a little, and I really think it makes a difference, even when she doesn't know me. And I still keep hoping, you know. I still believe that sooner or later she'll come back to me."

"Terribly expensive, those places, aren't they?" Judith said.

"But worth it, every bit of it!" he exclaimed. "The room she's in is really very pretty and cheerful and the nurses are splendid. Such patience, such understanding. If you have the vocation, it must be a wonderful thing to be a nurse."

"I used to be one myself," Judith said, "but I've never worked with mental cases. I don't think I'd have the understanding to do it."

"I've a feeling you would," he said, taking a long look into her eyes. "You give me the feeling you're one of the people who can share other people's suffering. That's the main thing."

She shook her head with a laugh. Her fingers still toyed with her topaz.

"I've enough to put up with on my own." But she said it lightly, as if it had no particular meaning. "If I go back to nursing, it'll be just because I want a job, that's all. How long has your wife been ill, Mr. Nixey?"

"About four years now," he answered, "though, looking back, I can see the signs were there much earlier than that. But I didn't pay much attention to them. I thought she was just getting a bit absent-minded and developing a few eccentricities as she got older, that perhaps it had something to do with not having had children and so on. When we got married she was very keen to have children and it was a dreadful disappointment when they told her she couldn't."

"I'm glad I haven't got any children," Judith said with a sudden flat bitterness in her voice. "It's one of the few really lucky things that have happened to me."

He looked astonished, as if he had never dreamt that any woman could say such a thing.

"Well, perhaps there are compensations," he said uncertainly. "I used to try to convince my wife that there were and get her to take up something seriously, like her music, for instance. She's very musical. It's one of the few things she still seems to respond to sometimes. But as I was saying, it's about four years since she broke down completely, and I thought at the time I'd have to give up my job to look after her. I couldn't bear the thought of letting her go into one of those awful National Health places. I suppose they're better than nothing, but there's no privacy, no individual care. Then Guy—Dr. Lampard—discovered Manstead

House, which solved all my worst problems. Have you met Dr. Lampard, Mrs. Partlett?"

"Yes," she said.

"Oh yes, of course, you and your husband are old friends of his, aren't you? He's a remarkable man, isn't he? I told him I was going to have to give up my job, but he wouldn't hear of it. Told me to take my time to make all the arrangements I needed, found out about Manstead House—oh, he helped me in every way. But he'd hate anyone to realize that that's the sort of man he is, kind and generous and sympathetic. A really good man."

"Indeed?"

There was an edge on her voice, but Ernest Nixey did not seem to notice it.

"Yes, I mean it," he said gravely. "And there aren't many people of whom I'd say it. A good man. Unkind sometimes because he doesn't always realize how he affects people. He can be a bit overpowering. But still he's just about the best man I've ever met."

Emma moved away. She joined Irene Carver and Colonel Branksome, who were talking about summer holidays, the colonel saying that there was no place like home and that he'd never go abroad if his wife didn't drag him away on terrible cruises, and Irene saying that the one thing she longed for in life was to travel, but how could you do that with three young children? Emma refilled their glasses and drifted on until she found herself next to Roger. He happened to be standing by himself at the moment, looking round the room with a troubled expression on his face.

"Have you noticed something a bit strange?" he said to her in a low voice. "Sam Partlett's vanished."

CHAPTER 4

Emma suggested that Sam had probably gone to the lavatory.

"If so, he's taking his time," Roger said.

"Did you see him leave?" she asked.

"No, I just noticed some time ago that he wasn't here."

"Perhaps he just got bored with us and left."

"That's possible."

"In any case, Judith seems quite happy. She's getting on very well with Ernest."

"You don't think she's noticed Sam's gone?"

"If she has, it doesn't seem to worry her. Of course, it may be the sort of thing she's used to. D'you think I should say anything to her about it?"

Roger glanced towards Judith. She had now separated from Ernest Nixey and was talking to Irene Carver. Maureen was trying to hold Bill Carver in conversation. Emma had noticed before that she seemed attracted to him, almost to the point of pursuing him, though as far as Emma could tell he had never given her any encouragement.

"I suppose we might as well wait a bit and see what happens," Roger said. "If he doesn't come back before she leaves you can hardly pretend you haven't noticed the fact, but for the moment there's no need to upset her."

"I think she's just noticed it herself," Emma said. "She's looking round."

Judith was still talking to Irene, but she was no longer showing the smiling interest of a moment before. Her gaze was roving about the room and there was an anxious frown on her forehead. After a little pause she became mute, making herself look back at Irene, but with the helpless sort of expression on her face of someone who is not taking in a word that is being said to her. With a desperate self-discipline she forced herself to start talking again and Emma heard her accepting an invitation to lunch one day the following week from Irene. Then presently, encountering Mrs. Branksome, Judith said that she was longing to join the W.I., but she was the first person to leave the party.

Emma went with her to the door, where Judith paused, fumbling in her handbag for the key of the flat upstairs.

"It's been such a nice evening—thank you so much," she said, like a little girl who has been taught that this is the right thing to say at the end of a party. "It was very kind of you to ask us. But I'm just a bit worried about Sam. I think perhaps he isn't feeling well and slipped out quietly because he didn't want to disturb anyone. But I think I ought to go up and see. Thank you again. You must come and have drinks with us one evening soon when we're more settled in."

She unlocked her door, went in and closed it behind her, then Emma heard her racing up the stairs as if a brake on her self-control had just been abruptly taken off.

Soon afterwards the party dissolved, the Branksomes leaving next, then the Carvers. Ernest Nixey was the last to go. He wanted to stay and help Emma with tidying the room and doing the washing up. He was a naturally domesticated man and one of the things that he missed badly as a result of his wife's illness, Emma thought, was sharing the care of what had once been a pleasant home. He still lived in their bungalow on the outskirts of Crandwich, where he occasionally entertained with a rather pathetic fussiness, bringing out the best china and the silver that he and his wife had been given as wedding presents, but compared with the not unpleasant disorder that the place had had before what was called his wife's breakdown, it had a petrified neatness, as impersonal as a hotel. He knew how to keep it tidy but had lost the desire to make it human.

However, Emma did not want to do any tidying that evening. She was tired and said that Mrs. Hawse would cope with everything in the morning. Ernest kissed her on the cheek and drove off to Crandwich.

Helping themselves to a final drink each, Emma and Roger sat down side by side on the sofa, with his arm going round her and her leaning comfortably against him. The room felt unnaturally silent, as rooms do after parties. Furniture had been pushed into unfamiliar places and looked lost there. As always, at such times, there was a feeling of anticlimax.

"I wonder what did happen to Sam," Emma said. "The last I remember of him, he was having some sort of argument with Bill. It looked a bit heated and I started wondering if I ought to go and break it up when someone else spoke to me and I forgot about it."

"It's not our affair, anyway," Roger said. "You've done all you can for them."

He had only just spoken when the doorbell rang.

He swore, but went out to the front door and after a moment returned with Judith, dressed again in her flowered quilted dressing gown and with a soapy scent about her, as if she had just taken a bath.

"I'm so sorry, I don't want to disturb you," she said hurriedly as Emma got to her feet, "but I simply can't stand sitting there waiting, not knowing what's happened to him, or what state he'll be in when he gets home. I feel awful, bothering you again, but what *am* I to do?"

"Where do you think he may have gone?" Roger asked. "To one of the pubs?"

"Probably, don't you think? Where else is there?"

"I could go and look for him," he said. "It won't take me long."

"Oh, I can't possibly ask you to do that," she protested quickly, but not very firmly.

"It's all right, I'll go. But he hasn't gone off in your car, I suppose, because if he has he might be anywhere."

"I don't think he could have got it out of the garage with all the other cars in your drive," she said.

"I'll just make sure, then I'll go down to the White Hart and the Dolphin." He went out.

After a minute or two he came back to say that the car was in the garage and that he was setting out to see if Sam was in either of King's Weltham's pubs and that if he found him he would do his best to bring him back. Judith mumbled again that she really couldn't ask him to go, that it was so good of him and that she knew that she and Sam were a nuisance to everybody, then as he went out she sank down in a chair and hid her face in her hands.

To give herself something to do while they waited, Emma began to straighten the furniture. Judith lowered her hands and sat watching her.

After a little she said, "You needn't worry, we'll move out."

"Where to?" Emma asked.

"I don't know, but we can't go on doing this kind of thing to you."

Emma felt inclined to agree with her but said nothing.

"If you'll just put up with us for a little while, while I look for something else . . ."

"It's all right, we'll work something out."

"You're very kind."

"Perhaps you're upset this evening for no real reason," Emma said. "Perhaps this kind of party just bores Sam. I don't altogether blame him."

"If I were you, I'd blame him for his discourtesy, if nothing else," Judith answered.

"I gave it mainly for you. I wasn't thinking of him. I wanted you to meet a few people."

"I know you did. As I said, you're very kind. It isn't everyone who'd bother."

"If Sam didn't want to stay around, it doesn't matter. And I expect Roger will bring him home in a few minutes."

But of course it did matter, because of the look of apprehension in Judith's eyes, and when Roger returned after about a quarter of an hour he did not bring Sam Partlett with him.

"Not in the White Hart or the Dolphin," he said, "and hasn't been in either at all this evening. It looks as if he's just gone for a walk, though it's hardly the weather for it. There's a nasty drizzle and the wind's getting up. But is that the kind of thing he does?"

"Sometimes," Judith said. "He likes walking by himself. He generally walks to the lab and back."

"Perhaps that's where he's gone," Emma suggested. "Has he some work going he might want to take a look at?"

"I don't know. I don't know much about his work." Judith stood up, pushing her curly hair back from her face. "In any case, it probably isn't anything to worry about. I wish I hadn't lost my head and come rushing down. I don't know why I did, exactly. I promise I won't do it again. I don't usually plague other people with my problems. It's just that sometimes one's got to talk to somebody. And you don't know how grateful I am to you for not giving me advice. Advice only makes one muddled and angry. One's got to deal with things by oneself, even if one only goes on and on making fearful mistakes." She went towards the door. "Good night. I really won't burst in on you again."

"Come any time you want to," Emma said.

"Thank you, but I really won't. Good night."

Roger saw her to the door. They heard the sound of her door open and close and of her footsteps on the stairs.

Coming back, Roger picked up the drink that he had left

behind when he set out on his search, sat down on the sofa and once more wrapped an arm round Emma as she settled down again beside him.

"In my view, that's a young woman who's near the edge of a crack-up," he said. "If you aren't careful, I think you may suddenly find your hands full."

"Another of King's Weltham's dotty wives," she said. She settled her head on his shoulder. "D'you know, I heard Ernest telling her all about his wife? He seemed to be rather attracted by her. D'you think he's one of the people who's unconsciously drawn to the mentally unstable?"

"Quite likely. He's a bit negative himself. He may like people who make him feel strong and capable."

"But he was also telling her what a perfectly wonderful man Guy is. I don't think she liked it much."

He drank some of his brandy. "Emma, I've got an appointment with Guy at four o'clock tomorrow afternoon. I'm going to tell him I'm going to Adelaide."

She stirred slightly in his embrace but did not lift her head from his shoulder.

"So you've made up your mind," she said quietly.

"Come with me," he said.

"Will you still go if I say I won't?"

"Probably."

"A few days ago you said you wouldn't."

"I've been having second thoughts."

"Why?"

"We've been over that so often. This is a dead end for me. If I stay here I'm going to decay. And you'll never come to the point of making up your mind how much you want me. You won't come to any decision. You'll go on and on, putting it off. And then one day we'll find it's too late and that neither of us minds much longer what happens to the other."

"I don't see why that should happen. I can love you as much here as I could in Adelaide."

"I wonder. There's a peculiar difficulty here."

She withdrew from him, settling herself against the far end of the sofa.

"I know what you're going to say," she said. "We always come to it sooner or later. You mean Guy."

He did not answer at once, then, gazing down into his drink, he said, "I've never asked you this. Have you ever slept with him?"

"Once," she answered.

"Why only once?" he asked.

"We both realized it wasn't what we wanted."

"But you still hold on to him. You've no confidence in yourself without him. You feel he's made you what you are."

"Perhaps he has."

"Then the best compliment you could pay him in return would be to show that you can stand on your own feet."

"I know. But can I?"

"Why not risk it?" There was a silence, then he repeated softly, "Come with me."

She drew a long breath, almost ready to give him the answer that he wanted but feeling a stab of panic as she realized what she was about to do, that in another moment she would be agreeing to change the whole course of her life, but as she hesitated the sound of a car on the gravel of the drive outside made her turn her head sharply. A car door slammed. Then stumbling footsteps crossed the outer hall to the door of the upper flat, the latch clicked as a key turned in it and the footsteps went on up the stairs. The car drove away.

"That's Guy's car," Roger said. "He's brought Sam home."

"So that's where he went—to see Guy," Emma said.

"But why did he go?"

As he spoke there was the sound of running footsteps overhead, a crash as if a chair had been knocked over, then a shrill scream.

"Oh, Christ, not again!" Roger said furiously, some of his blaze of anger coming because he realized that he had lost his hold on Emma at a moment when she had been about to yield to him.

She had sprung up and was making for the bureau where she kept the spare key to the flat above.

"We've got to stop them!" she cried. "We can't let it happen like last time."

"Wait!" He stood up, listening, his eyes on the ceiling above.

After the scream there was complete silence. There was not even the sound of anyone walking about. Roger and Emma waited. The silence continued. Emma found something eerie in it and realized suddenly that she was holding her breath.

At length Roger said dryly, "Let's hope it doesn't start up again. But d'you know, I think I'll go home. We can go back to what we were talking about some other time."

Emma drove to the Institute at the usual time next morning, sat down at her desk and resumed work on her paper. It had been coming along fairly well for the last few days and she thought that there was a chance that she might reach the end by the evening. Only of the first draft, of course. She knew that she would have to rewrite it from start to finish. And before she did that she wanted to show it to Guy and discuss it with him. Then, as she thought of that, she remembered what Roger had said about her dependence on Guy and so began to wonder if there was far more truth in that than she had ever wanted to face. The result of this was that she sat staring for a long time at a blank sheet of paper, then got up, put her coat on again, went out to her car and drove home.

Picking up her telephone, she rang up her hairdresser and made an appointment for the afternoon. Then she wandered about the flat, which had already been cleaned by Mrs. Hawse, sat down at her bureau and started signing cheques in payment of some bills that she had allowed to accumulate. From time to time she sat back in her chair and listened. She wanted to hear occasional footsteps overhead. That would have seemed normal. But there was only silence.

She felt a nagging desire to go to the Partletts' door and ring the bell and see if anyone answered. If one of them did, she could say that she was going into Crandwich that afternoon and ask if there was any shopping that she could do for them. There would be no need to show that she had been anxious. But what was she to do if no one answered?

She could hardly use her spare key to let herself into the flat to make sure that all was well there, when for all she knew the Partletts had simply gone out to lunch together in Crandwich, or perhaps were shopping for another pendant or some such thing. And what could she say if they came back and found her snooping?

Doing her best to ignore the silence, she presently went to the kitchen, made a sandwich and some coffee and, when she had finished them, got back into her car and drove to her hairdresser.

She did not often take days off in this fashion in the middle of the week. Her habit was to work fairly regular hours and to stay at home only at the weekend. But somehow she had to cope with the problem that Roger had set her the evening before, recognizing that her whole future depended on her answer. At the back of her mind she knew quite well what the answer was going to be, yet every time that she tried to commit herself to it a mood of panic returned. Life had been so simple as long as Roger had been satisfied with things as they were, but that happy state was not likely to return and what he was demanding of her now was that she should change her whole way of life. Perhaps it would have been easy if she had been young, but she had worked steadily, and had enjoyed it, for nearly twenty years, and she found the prospect of idleness and freedom terrifying.

Sitting under the hair dryer was soothing. The girl who always did her hair for her had far worse problems than Emma had ever had to contemplate. She had boy friends who abandoned her, boy friends who were too pressing, an aged mother who had recently taken to gambling and stole money for the purpose from her daughter's handbag, and a terrier bitch that had carelessly been allowed to become pregnant. The girl almost wept when she thought of what might have to be done to the puppies when they were born.

Emma did her best to say consoling things and felt better for the effort. It made her feel better too to look at herself in the mirror and see her grey hair artfully drawn back from her face and smoothly coiled up at the back of her head. If she was going to accept Roger's proposal of marriage, she thought with a faint smile at her reflection, she might as well look her best for it. Tipping the girl and paying her bill, she returned to her car and drove back to King's Weltham.

When she reached her laboratory she glanced at the electric clock on the wall. The time was twenty minutes past three. That meant that she was in plenty of time for a cup of tea. In another few minutes Mrs. Fallow and Dawn would be taking the tea urn and the biscuits into the common room. Emma decided to go along to it and then, if Roger came in, to tell him that she wanted to speak to him and suggest that they should go straight home.

Then she remembered that he had an appointment with Guy at four o'clock at which he intended to tender his resignation.

So the matter of their private lives would have to wait for a little. A pity, but there it was. A sharp sense of excitement, for which she was not prepared, invaded her. She felt almost scared of the thought of meeting Roger in the common room, where they had been meeting almost every day for seven years, yet at the same time she could hardly bear the thought of having to wait the next few minutes, until she could set off down the passage.

She was just turning to the door to go to the common room when the door opened and Sam Partlett came in.

Perhaps her face showed how little she wanted to see him just then, for he said, "I'm sorry—is this inconvenient? I just wanted to call in and apologize."

His face was paler than usual, with the slight puffiness that suggested a hangover.

"About last night?" Emma said. "Don't bother about it."

"But I do bother. I don't want you to think I don't." He gave his harsh smoker's cough. "I know it was discourteous. But the fact is, I was afraid that if I stayed something worse might happen. It was that man Carver. He hates the sight of me and wants me to know it and won't leave me alone. He was doing his best to make me lose my temper. And you know what I'm like when that happens. I could have ruined your party."

It was the nearest that he had come to referring to the evening when Judith had come fleeing to Emma for protection.

"Yes, well, there's no need to worry about it," Emma said, wanting to escape.

But now that he had started, he wanted to go on. "He'd got hold of the story of what I did the other evening. I think he got it from Hawse. He didn't say anything directly about it, but he started talking about the extraordinary things some women will put up with and looking at me in that damned sneering way of his to make sure that I knew what he was talking about. I could feel I was going to lose control in another moment, so I got out. At first I just meant to go for a walk and calm down and come back again, but then I got to thinking and in the end I went to see Guy. I wanted to tell him this business of coming to King's Weltham wasn't going to work and that the sooner I got out the better."

"You mean you're actually thinking of leaving?" Emma said, astonished. "Already?"

"Well, no." He looked embarrassed. "That was what I had in mind when I went to see Guy, but he talked me out of it. We had a few drinks and he got me to agree to give things a longer trial. I'm not sure I shouldn't have stuck to my point, but he's very persuasive, you know, when he wants to be."

"Then he drove you home, didn't he?" Emma said.

"You heard that, did you? And what happened too when I got in. Well, let me tell you, Judith sometimes gives as good as she gets. She's just about as strong as I am and she was in a tearing fury with me last night because she said I'd been rude to you."

"So it was you we heard scream, was it?" Emma said dryly. "I thought it was a woman."

"Oh, she screams at the least thing, sometimes just out of temper." His grey eyes, under his sandy eyebrows, surveyed her anxiously. "Don't you believe me?"

"I'm not sure I care much which of you it was. You both seem equally bent on making a hash of your lives."

"You don't much like us, do you?"

"Can you give me any reason why I should?"

He gave the charming smile that so transfigured his face and that made her wonder how she could ever have thought him colourless.

"I like you—isn't that a reason?" he said. "I haven't taken much to most of the people here, but I do like you. And Judith thinks you're wonderful."

"But I don't like couples who go in for punch-ups in the middle of the night, whichever of them is to blame," Emma said.

"It isn't an everyday occurrence, you know. It was just bad luck that things blew up last week. It's literally some years since it happened last."

"Since you last saw Guy?"

He raised his eyebrows, startled. "Perhaps it was. I can't really remember. It's a long time, anyway."

"How often has it happened altogether?"

"Oh, God knows. Of course, if Judith had any sense, she'd leave me. She tried it once or twice, but she always comes back."

"Isn't that because you threaten that if she doesn't you'll kill yourself?"

"But of course I shouldn't, and she knows that."

"I thought you did try it once. I thought that was how you met each other."

He shrugged his shoulders. "I'm afraid I've got a great love of drama. Actually when I did it I knew Guy would be coming into the room in a minute or two, but he was a bit later than I expected, so things nearly went wrong. It was utterly terrifying, but interesting too. I know what it feels like to hang between life and death."

"So it was a fake, was it?"

"Yes and no. Less, I think now, than I convinced myself immediately after it."

She looked at him thoughtfully, wondering how much of what he had said to believe.

"What was supposed to be your motive?" she asked.

"Oh, just *Weltschmerz*."

"And what was your real motive?"

He took a moment to answer. "Perhaps an experiment with death. Here we all are in a place like this, all as busy as bees with every sort of experiment, yet the one thing we don't think of investigating is the ultimate question."

"I doubt if any of us have the necessary qualifications to do that."

"Oh, all of us, all of us. We've each had one death allocated to us."

"What about your effort having been just a simple desire to make an impression on Guy and others?"

"Of course, that's probably right."

"I've been told you nearly killed a woman the night before you did it."

"Well, yes, that had something to do with it. Guilt gives one a craving for punishment. Have you ever suffered from any serious feelings of guilt?"

She was beginning to say that of course she had, that everyone had at some time in their lives, when she began to wonder if this was true in the sense in which he meant it. She had felt remorse for small, cruel acts, mainly due to stupidity rather than to any serious ill will. She had felt shame for blunders due to selfishness or insensitivity. But she had never felt that anything that she had done required that she should knot a rope round her neck.

"Let's go to tea," she said.

"Tea, by all means." He grinned. "All right, let's go."

He stood aside, holding the door open for Emma to go out ahead of him.

They went to the common room, past the doors that had the names of Ernest Nixey and William Carver on them, and past Arthur Hawse's glassed-in office, in which he was sitting reading a magazine, a fact which indicated that he had got back from having his tea with Mrs. Fallow and the technicians in the room that was so much more cheerful than the rather bleak room used by the scientific staff.

It was fairly full at the moment. One of the first people Emma saw was Roger, who happened to be looking at his watch as she came into the room. It made her automatically look at her own watch. It was ten minutes to four.

She wondered if Roger was being assailed now by feelings of misgiving. When it came to the point would he suddenly find that he did not want to give in his resignation after all and think of some other matter to discuss with Guy, such as the possibility of obtaining a new research grant, or any other relatively innocuous subject? His expression was no more tense than usual, as if he had nothing important on his mind. But that never meant anything with Roger. Emma was so accustomed to his faint, deceptive look of diffidence that she would only have thought about it if it had been absent.

Maureen Kirby brought her a cup of tea. She was wearing one of her tight jerseys and voluminous skirts that emphasized her opulent size.

"That was a lovely party you gave the other evening, Dr. Ritchie," she said. "I did enjoy it."

Emma thought that in reality the girl must have found it extremely dull. Except for herself, all the guests had been middle-aged and married. If she really had enjoyed the evening it could only have been that she had not enough friends of her own age and perhaps was lonely. It occurred to Emma that she knew next to nothing about Maureen's background, that she did not even know where she lived except that it was somewhere in Crandwich, from which she arrived in the mornings in a bright red Mini, the littleness of which, when she came billowing out of it, always made her look even larger than usual.

"Thank you," Emma said. Then with the feeling that often came to her of feeling sorry for the girl, she added, "You must come again. Perhaps I can find some guests of your own age."

"Oh, I like older people," Maureen said. "I like people who've had some real experience of life and don't pretend to know everything when really nothing's happened to them yet. As a matter of fact, I like really old people. I loved Colonel and Mrs. Branksome."

She sounded as if she meant it, yet she said it with an overeagerness that Emma found pathetic. She thought too that there was a look of strain on Maureen's bland pink face which was unusual. Or was it just that Emma had never troubled to notice it before? She wondered if perhaps Guy had just had one of his fits of bad temper and been unkind to the girl. And if that was the sort of mood he was in, how would he receive Roger?

"Do you live by yourself in Crandwich?" she asked. "It isn't your home, is it?"

"Well, it is and it isn't," Maureen answered. "My mum and my dad are in London and I go there most weekends, but in Crandwich I live with my gran. That's how I came to get my job here. I was visiting her when it was advertised. I've always spent a lot of time with her, even when I was a child, because Mum's a buyer for a big firm of drapers and has to travel a lot and so does my dad—he's a sales representative for a firm of confectioners." She gave a giggle. "Sometimes I think that's why I'm the size I am. I'm always eating up his samples. But Gran's a darling and wonderful for her age. You'd never think she was seventy-five. She's got a darling little bungalow the other side of Crandwich. I'm ever so lucky, really, having somewhere nice to stay instead of having to go into dreary old lodgings."

Emma nodded understandingly. But what it came to, she thought, was that Maureen had never had any real home life except what had been provided in snatches by her grandmother. Perhaps that explained her aura of unhappiness, which was so at odds with the first impression that she gave of fresh, healthy youth. In the circumstances an employer less complex than Guy, with his moods and his irony, would probably have been far better for her.

Once more Emma saw Roger glance at his watch. He was going to be punctual for his appointment with Guy, whatever it was that he intended to say to him.

Sam Partlett had sat down in a corner of the room by himself. He did not look as if he wanted to talk to anyone, or as if he meant to stay any longer than it took him to drink his cup of tea. But after a minute or two Ernest Nixey went over to him and started a conversation. Bill Carver watched this happen with a sardonic look on his face, then turned to Emma.

"I believe I ought to apologize to you, Emma," he said. "I believe I'm responsible for chasing your friend Partlett out of your house last night. I didn't mean to. I thought we were getting on rather well, chatting about this and that, when he turned his back on me and walked out. If it was my fault, I'm sorry."

"Oh, Bill, why don't you stop pretending?" Emma said, sipping her tea. "I don't know what you said to him, but you hate the man and you let him see it. It won't do you any good, you know. He's here to stay and you'd better get used to the idea."

"You think he's here to stay, do you?" Bill said. "I don't."

"Why not?"

"Because of something his wife said to Irene last night. Irene's asked her to lunch, incidentally, which is a bit of a nuisance because, while I've nothing against the woman, it'll be a bit difficult to be friendly with her if we don't want to have anything to do with her husband. But Irene likes giving lunch parties for wives. She says she has no social life here and that she'd die of boredom if she didn't do something of that sort occasionally."

"I don't think you need worry," Emma said. "Judith won't ask her back and the thing will die of itself."

"Why shouldn't she ask her back?" Bill demanded, sounding as if he took that as an insult.

"Her home life is a bit difficult," Emma replied. "It isn't the kind to encourage her to be hospitable. But what did she say to Irene to make you think they might not be staying?"

"Well, it was nothing much really. It was just that Sam never stays anywhere for long and that she herself has never cared for living in the country. She'd like to go back to London and get a job in one of the big hospitals. Irene thought she had a feeling that, if she had a job that would keep the two of them, it wouldn't matter much to her what Sam got up to."

"That may be just wish fulfilment on Judith's part," Emma said. "It sounds like it to me."

"Then you think he'll stay?"

"For a time, anyway."

"I suppose you're right." He looked across the room at Sam Partlett in his corner, with Ernest Nixey talking to him with his usual anxious friendliness, desperately needing companionship of any kind in his lonely life, while Sam had the air of wondering irritably how he could escape. "I don't think I've any obligation to encourage him to stay, however. Ernest can be friends with him if he wants to. Ernest's friends with everyone, even Lampard. And that reminds me of something I want to ask you, Emma. As long as Lampard's here, he's going to block my chances of getting ahead. He's made that pretty clear to me recently. I didn't get that job that Partlett got, which Lampard practically promised me when I came to work here. He told me Bushell would be retiring soon and that of course that would mean there'd be a vacancy, and I can't say he actually guaranteed it to me, but somehow it was in the air that that was what he meant. So I came here, but after the first few months, when all was rosy, I've run into nothing but frustration. I suppose I got across him somehow, but there are no research grants coming my way, no prospects, and that job I counted on went to that pal of his, Partlett. So now I'm thinking of looking for a job elsewhere, but the worst of it is that when I apply I'll have to give Lampard as a reference. That's what I want to ask you about. Do you think he'll do the decent thing and give me a fairly favourable write-up, or will he just seize the opportunity to kick me in the teeth?"

"I wish people didn't think I could read Guy's mind," Emma said.

"Then you don't think I can count on him to support me?"

The trouble was that Emma did not. She simply did not know how Guy might act. She knew that he had taken a dislike to Bill Carver, mainly because of Bill's very high opinion of himself, but whether Guy would go so far as to spoil Bill's chances of advancement, if any came along, was something about which she did not feel sure. There was a streak of the utterly capricious in Guy, which could make him as irresponsibly unkind as he could sometimes be generous.

"I don't really think he'd try to damage you," she said. "When it comes to assessing anyone's work, he's reasonably detached."

Roger stood up. For a moment his eyes met Emma's, then he crossed the room and went out.

"Of course, what he doesn't like about me is that I've never licked his boots," Bill said. "But he might be glad to get rid of me—"

It was at that point that the screams started.

They were a woman's screams, appallingly piercing, and they came from the direction of the staircase that led up to Guy Lampard's office.

For an instant there was shocked silence in the common room. Then there was a stampede towards the door. Someone jolted Emma's arm, so that her tea splashed on the floor. Managing to put her cup down, she went out with the others and stood at the bottom of the staircase, staring up.

Guy's door was open and in the doorway stood a thin woman, dressed in black, whom Emma had never seen before. It was she who was screaming. But as the crowd emerged from the common room, she thrust both hands against her mouth and forced back the shrieks, though she stayed where she was in the doorway, swaying.

Arthur Hawse was halfway up the stairs, going up them two at a time. Someone tried to hold Emma back, but she ran up after Arthur, then wished that she had not, for what she saw in Guy's room was the most fearful sight that she had ever seen in her life.

He was at his desk, slumped sideways in his chair, his head

hanging at a strange angle, with a great gash from ear to ear in his throat from which blood had gushed all over his chest and was still oozing in a bright crimson stream. Roger stood still behind him. There was blood on his hands and in his right hand was an open, bloodstained razor.

CHAPTER 5

Arthur Hawse came running down the stairs again as fast as he could, darted into his office and snatched up the telephone to call the police.

Roger stood staring at Guy, seemingly unconscious of the razor in his hand. Then he put it down on the desk and came towards the door, his bloodstained hands held out before him. The woman in black shrank back, as if he were about to lay them on her. He looked at her blankly. He might not have noticed her before. Standing still in the doorway, he addressed the crowd that had gathered in the hall and on the stairs.

"We'd all better go back into the common room and wait there till the police get here," he said.

He took a step forward.

"But your hands!" Ernest Nixey cried. He was standing beside Emma.

"Oh," Roger said, looking at them. "Yes. Just a minute."

He walked round the woman in black, went up the short flight of stairs from the half landing to the passage that led past Maureen's office and the library to his laboratory and disappeared along it.

People milled about in the hall for some minutes before they began to move back into the common room. Arthur Hawse came back to the door of his office and stood watching, making it clear that he meant to keep an eye on things.

Emma touched the strange woman on the arm. She spun round, looking as if she might start screaming again. She seemed to be about fifty but was so emaciated that she might well have been a younger woman who had withered early. Her pointed face was all sharp angles. It was extremely pale, though whether this was its normal condition or the result of what she had seen would have been hard to tell. She had heavy green make-up round her eyes and dark lipstick on her mouth. Her hair was a bright, unnatural red and was half covered by a black chiffon scarf.

"Do you mind telling me who you are?" Emma said.

"I'm Mrs. Fielding—Annette Fielding." The woman had a deep, throaty voice. "I was coming to see him—Dr. Lampard. And I walked into—this."

"You know him—knew him—did you?" Emma said.

"Certainly I knew him," the woman answered. "For very many years and very intimately."

"Was he expecting you?"

"Of course."

If that was true it appeared that Guy had made appointments with two people for the same time, but this had not been beyond him.

"Well, perhaps it would be best if you came downstairs with us," Emma said. "We'll all have to wait for the police."

"But that man—that murderer!" the woman said, pointing after Roger. "Aren't you going to do anything about him?"

"I don't think he's the murderer," Emma said. "He went into the room only a moment before you."

"It doesn't take long to cut a throat." The woman spoke with a disconcerting air of knowledgeability. "And with so much blood about, poor Guy can only have been dead for a few minutes. If I hadn't been so close behind the man he could have got away."

"Let's leave that to the police." Emma took a firmer hold of Mrs. Fielding's arm and drew her down the stairs.

It bewildered her that this woman had had any part in Guy's

life. She knew that he had had occasional affairs with women, but for some reason she had always assumed that they would all have been young, exuberant and, above all, casual. That this skeletal person had apparently been there in the background over the years and that he had never even mentioned her existence to Emma seemed very strange. But perhaps her relationship with him had not been sexual, though that was what she had seemed to imply. Perhaps she was a relative, or a connection by marriage. Emma knew surprisingly little about his family, except that all of them, including Guy, were fairly wealthy and that he had always seemed to do his best to avoid them.

Feeling for Guy was just beginning to come alive in Emma. At first she had been so numbed by shock that she had felt no sense of grief or loss. But gradually she began to become aware of what his death would mean to her. Ever since she grew up he had always been there. He had helped her from the beginning. She had an immense debt of gratitude to him. And of course Roger had been right when he said that she had deeply depended on him. What she would have made of her life if he had not been there to encourage her, direct her, sometimes bully her, was something that she could not estimate. At times he had been intolerable, but on the whole, after a fashion, she had loved him.

At the moment it was that that suddenly struck her, giving her a sense of almost unbearable pain. But this was not the time to show it. In the silent common room, where people stood about in small groups, most of them looking pale and scared, she kept her attention on Mrs. Fielding.

Maureen approached her.

"Would you like some tea?" she asked. "I'm afraid this is cold, but we could get some more."

"No, thank you—please don't trouble," the woman answered. She had sat down on the edge of a chair with her hands folded tightly together in her lap. She did not look at Emma but stared straight before her. "I suppose I must wait here. I'm staying at a hotel in Crandwich. The police could find me there if they want me. I—I find it very difficult to sit here among all these strange people and not give way. I should like to leave."

"I think it would be best to stay for the present," Emma said. "I expect the police will let you go if you can satisfy them that you came into the building after Dr. Challoner started up the stairs."

"They won't, you know. They'll ask me questions and questions and questions!" The woman's voice went up, quavering and shrill.

"Do you think the porter saw you come in?" Emma asked.

"Certainly he did. We said good afternoon to one another."

"You didn't ask him the way to Dr. Lampard's office?"

"There was no need for me to do so."

"Then you've been here before?"

"Of course. Frequently."

Emma was puzzled. If Mrs. Fielding had had the sort of close relationship with Guy that she seemed to want Emma to recognize, why was she staying in a hotel in Crandwich instead of in Guy's house? Guy's housekeeper, aged Dorothy, might have objected to her and Guy had always been very considerate of Dorothy's feelings. She was the one person who had always been able to scold him ferociously without getting worse than she gave. But if Mrs. Fielding had been his mistress for years, surely Dorothy must have known of it and become reconciled to it.

It piqued Emma slightly that she had known nothing of it herself.

"How did you get here?" she asked. "By taxi?"

"By car," Mrs. Fielding answered. "I drove down to Crandwich from London, then drove on here after I'd booked in at the George. My car's in the car park at the side of the building. I suppose that was the right place to put it. Oh, God, here's that terrible man! I shall start screaming again if he comes near me."

She had turned her head to stare at the door. Roger had just come in. He had washed his hands in his laboratory but was holding them away from his sides, as if he felt some stain might be clinging to them.

"I think one of us should stay out here with Arthur," he said, "so that the police won't be able to bother him about whether or not he left his office."

He spoke in a tone of authority, which reminded Emma that he was deputy director of the Institute, a fact that she was inclined to forget, and that for the time being he was in charge here.

"Quite right," Ernest Nixey said. "I'll go."

He left the room hurriedly. Then he came back into it.

"The police are here already," he said. "Roger, you'd better come and talk to them."

Only one police car had arrived, with a sergeant and a constable in it. With the door of the room left open, Emma heard their voices and Roger's in the hall, then these faded as they went up the stairs together. Then more cars arrived and more policemen invaded the building. Becoming aware that her temples were throbbing and that she was feeling sick, Emma began to wish that there was something stronger to drink in the place than cold tea. In her own room she could at least have made some hot coffee, which would have been better than nothing, but one of the policemen had come into the room to ask everyone to stay there until Detective Superintendent Day decided what steps were to be taken next, so it was impossible to leave.

Mrs. Fielding had subsided in her chair, putting one hand over her eyes. Emma could see that she was biting her lips, as if to stop them trembling. Maureen had drawn a chair up close to the woman and seemed, in a low voice, to be attempting to console her. Bill Carver had gathered a group of people around him and was telling them in a voice that sounded a little too loud for the occasion that murder was an abominable thing, that he was as shocked at it as anybody, but that nevertheless, if ever anyone had asked for it, it was Guy Lampard. Ernest Nixey had helped himself to a cup of tea from the urn and did not seem to mind the fact that it was cold. Sam Partlett had returned to the corner where he had been sitting earlier and had a cigarette dangling from between tight lips. There was an abstracted frown on his face, as if he were trying to chase down some thought that eluded him. Emma saw him give a little shake of his head as he apparently rejected one that had occurred to him, then he noticed her watching him and, frowning more deeply, turned his head away so that she could not see his eyes. Time passed extremely slowly.

Detective Superintendent Day presently established himself in the library. It was a big room that had probably once been the drawing room of the mansion. There were several long tables in alcoves lined with books, three tall windows with their sills crowded with pot plants, the care of which was one of Maureen's hobbies, and a plentiful supply, attached to the old moulded ceiling, of fluorescent lights. The superintendent first interviewed Roger there, then Arthur Hawse, then sent a constable to ask Mrs. Fielding to come up to the library.

Roger had returned to the common room by then and had sat down beside Emma, but they did not speak, though when she gave him a questioning look he replied to it with a helpless little gesture which told her that he understood no more than she did. After a time Mrs. Fielding returned and Ernest Nixey was asked to go up to the library. Mrs. Fielding looked even whiter than before, if that was possible, dropped into a chair, covered her face with her hands and began to rock to and fro, making a strange moaning noise. In another moment, Emma felt, the woman might be tossing her head up and laughing wildly.

Standing up, Emma said, "I don't care what the police say, I'm going to take her to my lab and give her some coffee. We'll have a real fit of hysterics here if I don't do something of the sort."

"All right," Roger said. "I'll explain to them, if necessary."

Emma laid a hand on Mrs. Fielding's shoulder.

"Come along with me," she said. "We'll go along to my lab, where it's quiet."

"What?" Mrs. Fielding said. "Oh—oh yes, that'll be nice."

She got unsteadily to her feet and let Emma take her by the arm and guide her out of the room.

As they passed Arthur Hawse's office she saw him watching her with interest. Emma would have liked to ask him if he had ever seen the woman before, but this was hardly the time for that. If she had no opportunity to do so soon, she would probably be able to question him at home in the evening. Taking Mrs. Fielding into her laboratory, she led her to the chair at the desk and closed the door. Plugging in the electric kettle, she got two cups out of a cupboard and spooned coffee into them. It was only instant coffee, but she made it extra strong.

"I'm sorry, I've no milk or sugar," she said.

"That's all right, thank you. I don't take them." Mrs. Fielding suddenly sounded quite composed.

Emma put a cup down on the desk in front of her, then perched on one of the stools, sipping her own coffee. Glancing at the clock on the wall, she saw that the time was twenty-five minutes to six. It was an hour and a half since Roger had discovered the murder, but it felt far longer than that. Outside it was dusk and the room was almost dark, but she felt reluctant to turn on the very bright lights overhead which would show up vividly the suffering on the other woman's face.

"You'll think me a fool," Mrs. Fielding said in the same calm way after she had drunk some coffee, "going to pieces like that in front of everyone—no self-control. I'm afraid I'm a very emotional person. I'm easily upset. It was thoughtful of you to take me away from all those people. I could feel them all staring at me, even when they were pretending not to. I suppose they all guessed about Guy and me. You knew about it, of course."

"Actually, I didn't," Emma answered. "But there's no need to talk about it."

"There's no reason why I shouldn't now. I've told the police all about it. Guy and I were lovers for years. We met first when we were quite young, but I was married and my husband wouldn't divorce me, and anyway, Guy wasn't a marrying sort of man. Even though I loved him deeply, I don't know that I could have borne living with him day in, day out. You knew him well, so I'm sure you'll know that I mean."

"I suppose I do," Emma said.

"But now that he's gone," Mrs. Fielding went on, "and so horribly too, I don't know how I'm going to face it. Yet I came down here to break things off, isn't that strange? I'm wondering now how I could ever have thought of doing such a thing."

"So that's why you went to a hotel instead of staying with him," Emma said. "I thought it might have been because of Dorothy."

"Dorothy?"

"His housekeeper."

"Oh yes, of course, I'd forgotten her name for the moment. No, it wasn't because of her, though on the whole we were careful to be discreet. But that was because of my husband. We never actually separated, because he's a cripple—polio, you know. It happened some time after I'd met Guy, when I'd almost made up my mind to go away with him, but then I felt I couldn't go, my husband needed me so badly. It annoyed Guy, because he wanted to be the only man in my life, but I couldn't bring myself to leave poor Reginald."

Emma felt a sudden impulse to turn on the light. She had begun to want to see the other woman's face, because she could not make herself believe the story she was being told. For one thing, no one who knew Guy could forget who Dorothy was.

She was embedded in his life as firmly as any parent. It was a relationship to which he had always been absolutely steadfast. And if Mrs. Fielding had wanted to put an end to her affair with Guy, why should she have come to the Institute to do it, and in the middle of the afternoon, instead of finding somewhere more private? And didn't the crippled husband fit into the story a little too conveniently? But why Mrs. Fielding should have wanted to tell the story, if it was not true, was puzzling.

Emma got down from her stool and went to the door and pressed the light switch beside it. The room was flooded with light, which for a moment seemed intolerably brilliant. She blinked and, as she did so, happened to notice the watch on her wrist. The time it showed was five minutes to six. That meant that she and Mrs. Fielding had been talking for twenty minutes. It did not seem nearly as long as that. Not really questioning the fact, yet feeling that she must check it, she looked at the clock on the wall and saw that the time it showed was only a quarter to six.

She stood still where she was, staring at the clock to see if it had stopped. She had never before known it to go wrong. But her watch was very reliable too. If it, rather than the clock, had been slow, she might have thought that she had forgotten to wind it and that it had almost run down, but it was unlikely that it had suddenly taken to galloping ahead. As she stood there, she saw the minute hand of the clock move onwards.

Mrs. Fielding was watching her. "What's the matter?" she asked.

"Nothing," Emma replied. "Do you happen to know what the time is?"

The woman thrust out a bony wrist and looked at the diminutive gold watch on it.

"Five minutes to six," she said.

So Emma's watch was right and it was the clock that was

wrong. Perhaps there had been a brief power cut. Not that it was important.

"Would you like some more coffee?" she asked.

"Please, if I may. It's a great help."

Emma plugged in the kettle again and spooned more coffee into both their cups.

"I believe you've been here a long time," Mrs. Fielding said.

"Seven years," Emma answered.

"Of course, Guy was devoted to you. He relied on you so much. You'd known him for a long time, hadn't you, before you came here?"

It irked Emma that Mrs. Fielding should appear to know so much about her when she had known nothing of the woman's existence.

"I was a Ph.D. student of his at London University," she said. "Altogether I knew him for about sixteen years."

"Almost as long as I did," Mrs. Fielding said with a sigh. "I'm sure you'll miss him terribly."

"I shall."

"But not everyone will. He wasn't the easiest of men to get on with."

"No."

"Lots of people didn't like him."

"No."

"Have you thought—have you begun to think—who could have done this unspeakable thing to him?"

Emma shrank from the question. It had been at the back of her mind, naturally, ever since she had seen Guy's bloodstained corpse and was something, she knew, that sooner or later would have to be faced. But not now. She could not try to be rational about it yet.

"That's the job of the police," she said.

"But someone like you, who knew so much about him, surely

you've some ideas." There was something very intense about the way Mrs. Fielding was looking at Emma.

The kettle was boiling. She made the coffee and gave Mrs. Fielding her cup again.

"As you've said, a lot of people didn't like him," Emma said, "but that's not a good enough motive for murder."

"You never can tell. Things can seethe away in people under the surface, things most of us wouldn't give a second thought to, and then suddenly they explode—" Mrs. Fielding broke off as the door opened.

Roger looked in.

"The superintendent wants you, Emma," he said.

"All right," she said, "I'll come. D'you want to stay here, Mrs. Fielding, or would you sooner go back to the other room?"

Mrs. Fielding put her cup down on the desk and stood up. "I suppose I'd better go back. Being alone just now perhaps isn't"— she gave a crooked smile—"advisable."

"If you like, I'll send Miss Kirby to you," Emma said. "Then you can stay here."

"Oh, that would be kind. Yes, I'd prefer that." The thin woman sank down on her chair again.

Emma and Roger returned to the common room where Emma asked Maureen to go and keep Mrs. Fielding company, which of course was a way of asking her to keep an eye on her, then she went upstairs to the library.

Detective Superintendent Walter Day was sitting at a table in one of the book-lined alcoves. Another man, whom he introduced to Emma as Sergeant Peters, was at the far end of the table with a heap of notes in front of him. Both men stood up when Emma entered and the superintendent gestured her to a chair facing him, then sat down again.

He was a tall, gangling man of about forty-five, with close-cropped grey hair, blue eyes set far apart above a short, blunt nose and a wide mouth with a slight downward curve that gave him a look of gentle melancholy. His brown suit hung on him loosely and was rather shabby. If Emma had met him in other circumstances, she would probably have guessed that he was an overworked general practitioner.

He asked for her name and address, how long she had worked at King's Weltham, where she had worked before and how well she had known Dr. Lampard. She gave him a brief account of her relationship with Guy, keeping it as impersonal as possible, and when he asked her if she had any ideas concerning the murder that she felt like volunteering, she shook her head.

"It was a complete shock to you, then," he said.

"Complete."

"What was the first you knew of it?"

His voice was low-pitched and soft. To Emma he seemed far too mild a man to be a policeman. She could far more easily imagine herself telling him her gynaecological symptoms than discussing clues to a murder.

"I was in the common room and I heard Mrs. Fielding screaming," she said. "We all ran out and I went about halfway up the stairs after Dr. Challoner and I saw into Dr. Lampard's office and saw him . . . Well, you know what I saw."

"Was anyone else in the room with him?"

"Yes, Dr. Challoner."

"What was he doing?"

"He was standing behind Dr. Lampard. He—" She stopped. "But he's told you all this himself."

"Just tell me in your own words," he said quietly. "I know it's very upsetting for you, but I want to get as complete a picture as I can. Was he holding anything?"

"Yes," she said reluctantly. "A razor."

"Was it open?"

"Yes."

"How might he have come by it?"

96

"I suppose he found it on the desk and picked it up without thinking. Wasn't it what was used to—to kill Dr. Lampard?"

"Possibly, but we haven't checked that yet. It's a pity Dr. Challoner picked it up. He may have smudged fingerprints. But when I asked you how he might have come by it, I really meant, where do you think it might have come from? Not many people use that kind of razor nowadays."

"You'll find razors like that in a number of labs in the building," Emma answered, "and there's a supply of them in a cupboard in one of the technicians' rooms. I've one of my own in my lab. We use them for section cutting."

He nodded and she realized that he had already been told this by some of the people before her.

"And where was Mrs. Fielding when you saw into the office?" he asked.

"In the doorway," Emma said.

"But you could see past her, could you?"

"Yes."

"Are you acquainted with her?"

"I'd never met her before, but I've just been talking to her. I understand she's an old friend of Dr. Lampard's."

She thought that she saw a sardonic gleam in his eyes, as if he were amused at her euphemism.

"Did you see her come in?" he asked.

"No," she said, "she was already on the landing when I came out of the common room."

"And what time was this?"

"Just four o'clock."

"Just four o'clock. You can be as exact as that, can you?"

"Yes, it happens I knew Dr. Challoner had an appointment with Dr. Lampard at four o'clock and I noticed him in the common room, keeping a careful check on the time. It was four o'clock when he went out."

"Do you know when he went into the common room?"

"No, he was already there when I went in."

"And what time was that?"

"I think it was about ten to four. Perhaps Mr. Hawse could tell you. He was in his office by the main entrance when I passed it. That means he'd got back from having his own tea. He's generally very punctual about it. He goes off duty from just three-thirty to three forty-five—Oh!" She stopped abruptly.

"Yes?" he said, as if he were asking her when the symptoms had first appeared. "You've just remembered something?"

"It probably isn't important," she said. "I don't know if it means anything. But it happens that the clock in my room is wrong. It's ten minutes slow. That means I'm not sure what time I went to the common room. It could have been later than I realized."

The superintendent was silent for a moment, looking at her thoughtfully, considering the implication of what she had said.

"When did you notice the clock was wrong, Miss Ritchie—" He glanced down at a paper before him and corrected himself. "Dr. Ritchie?"

"Only just before you sent for me," she said. "But it may have been wrong earlier, I don't know."

He turned to the sergeant.

"Get that checked, will you, Sergeant?" he said.

The sergeant went out, returning after a moment, presumably having sent some constable to look at the clock in Emma's room.

As he sat down again and resumed his note-taking. the superintendent went on, "Let's go back a little, Dr. Ritchie. You spent the afternoon in your lab, did you?"

"No," Emma replied, "I spent the morning there, then I went home for lunch, then I went into Crandwich to my hairdresser. That's Jennifer in the High Street. I only got back to my lab about twenty past three. At least, that's what it said on the clock. I happened to notice it because I was thinking I'd like a cup of tea before I started work, and I saw I'd ten minutes to wait before Mrs. Fallow would be bringing the tea along."

"You didn't look at your watch at the time?"

"No."

"But you think now it may really have been half past three already when you got back to your lab?"

"I don't *think* so," Emma said. "I don't think it would have taken me as long as that to get back from Crandwich. I don't drive particularly fast, but there wasn't much traffic."

"So you're inclined to think the clock went wrong later."

She nodded. "But is it important? Even if my clock was wrong, it doesn't mean anything special, does it?"

"It's hard to tell. At the moment we're just trying to check up where everyone was at the time Dr. Lampard was murdered. We can pinpoint that fairly accurately, apart from any medical evidence, by what Arthur Hawse has told us, always supposing that what he said is true. He says that at a few minutes before half past three he saw Miss Kirby come out of Dr. Lampard's office, come downstairs and go into the common room, that he then went away to have his own tea and returned punctually at a quarter to four, and that from then on no one went into Dr. Lampard's office until Dr. Challoner went up to it, followed a moment later by Mrs. Fielding, who had just come in at the main entrance. So supposing Dr. Lampard was alive when Miss Kirby left him—we haven't questioned her yet, but naturally she'll say he was—it seems certain that Dr. Lampard was killed between half past three and a quarter to four. Of course, there was a good deal of coming and going outside the common room during that time, so we've a good many people to interview, and it's possible Hawse's attention wasn't on Dr. Lampard's door all the time, even when he was there, so we can't be certain about anything yet, but those fifteen minutes are the time in which we're most interested."

Emma nodded again.

99

He went on. "Now will you tell me something, Dr. Ritchie? You say you noticed that when you got back from Crandwich the time was twenty minutes past three. Let's forget for the moment that the clock may have been wrong. You say you noticed it because you were looking forward to having a cup of tea and you saw you'd ten minutes to wait. So it sounds as if you really wanted that cup of tea. Yet you say it was about ten to four when you went to the common room. So in fact you waited half an hour before you went there. Was there any special reason for that?"

"Yes," she said, "I had a visit from Dr. Partlett."

"Ah, we haven't talked to him yet," he said. "What was the time when he came to see you?"

"It must have been about twenty-five minutes past three."

"Did he stay long?"

"For some time. We went along together to the common room."

"Which gives you both an alibi, unless of course . . ." He paused, frowning. "If your clock was ten minutes slow when you got back from Crandwich, then it wasn't three-twenty when you got in but three-thirty, and Dr. Partlett didn't come to see you at three twenty-five but at three thirty-five, which gives him time to have done the murder—just. Yes?"

The door had opened and a constable had come in.

"I've investigated the clocks downstairs, sir," he said, "and all the clocks in the rooms along the passage from the main hall to Dr. Ritchie's lab are ten minutes slow, except Mr. Nixey's. His secretary's, Miss Atkinson's, is slow, but not Mr. Nixey's, and as his is on the same circuit as the others', it seems unlikely there was a power cut. But there might be something wrong with the wiring. We're still looking into that."

The superintendent nodded and the constable withdrew.

"All the rooms along that passage," Walter Day said. "Whose rooms are they?"

"Dr. Partlett's, Dr. Carver's and Miss Atkinson's," Emma replied. "You reach Mr. Nixey's room through Miss Atkinson's. She's away at the moment with bronchitis."

"Well, we must look into it. Do you know anything of the relationship between Mr. Nixey and Dr. Lampard, Dr. Ritchie?"

"I think it was very good," she said. "I know Mr. Nixey had an immense respect for Dr. Lampard. I've heard him speak of him with the greatest admiration."

"I see. Thank you. I think I'd better speak to Dr. Carver next and see if he has anything to say about his clock. Sergeant, will you get him?"

The sergeant stood up, opened the door for Emma, then set out in search of Bill Carver.

Emma went downstairs, passing the closed door of Guy's office, from behind which she could hear voices and the sounds of several people moving about. They would be looking for fingerprints, she supposed, and taking photographs, and perhaps the police surgeon was there and soon men would come with a stretcher and an ambulance would come to the entrance. She shivered. It had been strangely easy to talk calmly to the superintendent, but now reaction was setting in and, though it did not show outwardly, inwardly she was shaking.

Going down the stairs to the hall, she hurried along the passage to her laboratory, thinking of it as a place where she could be alone for at least a few minutes to try to regain the self-control that she felt was slipping. Then she remembered that Mrs. Fielding and Maureen Kirby would be there, so it would be no refuge. She paused for a moment outside the door, drew a deep breath, went in and found that there was no one there.

Her first feeling was relief. Dropping into the chair at the desk, she sat there for some minutes, allowing herself to tremble. She saw Mrs. Fielding's coffee cup on the desk, with the arc of her lipstick on it and a mashed cigarette end in the saucer.

Emma's coffee cup was on the bench where she had left it. She thought of making herself some more coffee, found that the thought repelled her, longed for a stiff whisky and wondered how long it would be before she was allowed to go home.

Perhaps she could go now if she could find the right man to ask. In any case, the first person to consult was Roger. She stood up, driving her hands down into her pockets, fighting her trembling, then returned along the passage to the common room.

She expected, besides Roger, to find Maureen there with Mrs. Fielding. But Maureen was alone, sitting drooping in dejection on one of the plastic chairs. She turned her head quickly as Emma came into the room, got up and came towards her.

"She's gone," she said. "I went off to the toilet, telling her I'd be back in a minute, and when I came back she'd gone. I looked all round for her, but she'd simply vanished. And I looked out in the car park, because she'd said her car was there, but it was gone too. That's to say, there aren't any cars there I don't know. Do you think it matters? Is it my fault? I'm so sorry."

Emma said she supposed there was nothing that they could do about it, that no one had asked them to keep an eye on the woman and that what had happened was the responsibility of the police. They might even have told her that they no longer required her and allowed her to go back to her hotel. She looked round for Roger, but he was not in the room.

"D'you know where Dr. Challoner is?" she asked.

"He went up to his lab," Maureen said. "He told me to tell you, in case you came looking for him."

Emma returned up the stairs. The chill came back as she passed the closed door of Guy's office, but she went on up the stairs to the next landing and into Roger's laboratory.

It was a room very like her own, though less tidy. A litter of books and journals was scattered around. In the fume cupboard there were some disgestion flasks which were being heated for the estimation of nitrogen in the tissue of some apples. Roger was not alone. Stanley Rankin, the head technician, was with him. He was a small, spare man with a sombre, leathery face, scanty brown hair and very shrewd grey eyes. He had already been an institution at King's Weltham when Emma came to work here, having worked his way up from the lowliest of assistant technicians to his present very responsible position and become the man in the whole Institute on whom Guy had placed the most complete reliance. Sometimes Emma had felt that he knew Guy even better than she did.

The two men had the look, when Emma entered, of having been interrupted in an important and highly confidential discussion.

"I'm sorry," she said. "I'll come back presently."

"No, it's all right—come in," Roger said. "Stan's just been telling me something very disturbing."

What could be disturbing compared with what else had happened there that day Emma could not imagine, but she shut the door and perched herself on a stool.

"What is it?" she asked.

Stanley Rankin, who was normally a very quiet man, looked at Roger, leaving it to him to do the talking.

"Well, some days ago Stan spotted something rather peculiar going on," Roger said. "It seems our barbiturates have been vanishing at an abnormal rate. He isn't sure when it started, he thinks some time ago, but he only noticed it for sure last week. He realized he'd been signing order forms a good deal too often. So he's checked it carefully and he's quite certain that the stuff's disappearing in a way that's distinctly suspicious."

In the Institute barbiturates were used by some people in making buffer solutions for stabilizing acidity and could be obtained without any difficulty along with other scientific supplies.

"That might be serious," Emma said. "Did Guy know about it?"

"I told Dr. Lampard about it as soon as I was sure of it,"

Stanley Rankin replied. "He said leave it to him. He said he thought he knew who was taking the stuff and that he'd sooner sort it out himself on the quiet than have a big row about it. So I've done nothing. But I thought I'd better tell Dr. Challoner about it before I tell the police. Because that's what I've got to do, isn't it? Isn't that right? It might be something important."

"It might be something very important," Roger answered. "Of course you must tell the police."

CHAPTER 6

It was nearly half past eight when Emma reached home. The police had allowed everyone to leave by then, but Roger had disappeared. She thought that he and Stanley Rankin might have been kept behind to discuss the matter of the barbiturates. Putting her car into the garage, she went into her flat, poured out the whisky for which she had been longing for some time, switched on the electric fire and sat down beside it.

She was not in the least hungry, but thought that presently she would have to prepare a meal of some sort. But if she waited for a while Roger might arrive in time to share it with her, for surely he would join her as soon as he could. It would not be like him to leave her alone that evening.

Yet she was not ungrateful to be left by herself for a time. There was something healing about silence. Trying to remember Guy as the living man whom she had known for so long and not as the lifeless figure, slumped and bloodstained in his chair, she found that she could think of him now with grief and not only with shock and horror, and that that brought its strange kind of peace. Her thoughts wandered away to early memories of him, when his forcefulness had both intimidated and excited her, and it startled her acutely, bringing her back to herself too suddenly, when she realized that someone had just rung the doorbell.

Putting down the empty glass that she had been nursing for some time, she got up and went to the door. Judith Partlett stood there. She was in her quilted dressing gown and had her usual soapy scent, and her hair had a fluffy look, as if she had recently washed it. Emma found herself thinking that Judith must almost live in that dressing gown and must have a habit of taking baths and washing her hair whenever she was bored or lonely.

There was an anxious look on her face now as she gazed questioningly at Emma.

"Something's happened, hasn't it?" she said. "Something's wrong."

"You mean you don't know about it?" Emma said. "Sam hasn't come home yet?"

Judith shook her head, as if that in itself were not significant.

"But I heard you come in much later than usual," she said, "and Roger isn't here, and Sam—well, he phoned some time ago and said whatever anyone said to me I wasn't to worry and then he just rang off suddenly, as if he thought someone was listening to him and he didn't want them to hear what he was saying. And now that he hasn't come home I can't help wondering what he thought I might be worrying about. I expect he's in one of the pubs and he'll be in presently, but I've had a sort of feeling, ever since that call of his, that something's wrong. Do you know about it? Is it something he's done? Is it something awful?"

"It's awful, but I don't know that Sam's got anything to do with it," Emma said. "Come in and I'll tell you about it."

She took Judith into the living room, gave her a drink and helped herself to a second.

"Guy's dead," she said abruptly, feeling that there was no need to break that piece of news to Judith gently. She might be horrified, but she was not one of the people who would mourn. "He was murdered this afternoon. Someone got into his office and cut his throat with a razor from one of the labs. It probably happened between half past three and a quarter to four. The police have been in the place ever since it was discovered. That's why I got home late. They kept us there all the evening, answering questions. I think Roger may be with them still. I don't know if they've got anywhere by now, but perhaps he'll be able to tell us when he gets here."

She had expected Judith to take it calmly, but she was met with a wild, desperate stare. For a moment Judith pressed a fist against her mouth, as if she were trying to hold in a cry, then after all it escaped her. "Sam! That's why he telephoned! They suspect him! Oh, Sam!"

Emma felt the irritation of someone exposed to another person's hysteria when she is having some difficulty in keeping control of her own.

"I don't think there's any reason to suspect Sam," she said. "As a matter of fact, I believe I can give him a complete alibi. If the police are right that Guy was killed between three-thirty and three forty-five, Sam's absolutely in the clear. He came into my lab about three twenty-five and we stayed talking until about three-fifty, when we went along to the common room. Anyway, what motive could he possibly have for killing Guy?"

"Sam doesn't need a motive for what he does," Judith answered. She drank a little of her whisky, keeping her frightened eyes on Emma's face. "Killed!" she exclaimed. "His throat cut! Oh, God—Sam!"

"But I tell you, it couldn't have been Sam," Emma said impatiently. She did not think it necessary to mention the slight confusion introduced into the situation by the fact that her clock had been wrong.

"But how do you explain that extraordinary phone call?" Judith asked. "Wasn't he trying to tell me not to worry if he was suspected?"

"Don't worry, then," Emma said. "I expect he was in a pretty bad state of shock, as we all were, but it's probably hit him harder than anyone else, and he just wanted to talk to you. He probably didn't realize how odd it sounded. I honestly don't think there's any reason to think the police suspect him."

Judith let out a long breath and some of the tension went out of her body.

"I'm being stupid, of course," she said. "It's just that I've a way of always expecting the worst. It's a bad habit I've got into, living with Sam. How can the police tell so exactly when Guy was killed?"

"Well, Arthur saw Maureen come out of his office a little before half past three, when he went off to have his tea, so it seems probable Guy was alive then. I gather Maureen went straight into the common room, so she can't have had any bloodstains on her, so it doesn't seem likely she'd done a murder before she came down. And Arthur's also sure no one went up to Guy's room after he got back from having his tea until Roger went up at four o'clock."

"I suppose there were other people about in the hall during that time who might have seen who went up," Judith said.

"I should think there must have been," Emma answered. "That's probably why the police kept us so long, questioning everyone who could have been in the hall and seen anyone on the staircase."

"But you say Sam couldn't have been there."

Thinking of that clock, Emma hesitated, but then committed herself. "I'm sure he couldn't."

"Thank you for telling me that," Judith said.

"But two people who could have been there," Emma said, "were Bill Carver and Ernest Nixey. They both went along to the common room during the time Arthur was away."

"Are you telling me that one of them could be the murderer? Oh no, not Ernest, that isn't possible! He's the kindest little man alive. Think how good he is to that poor wife of his. Bill Carver —well, I don't much like him, but that doesn't mean he's a murderer. D'you know, I can see Maureen doing it more easily than Ernest or Bill. She gives me a queer feeling, that girl. There's something the matter with her. But you say it couldn't have been her." Judith stood up. "Has Roger an alibi?"

"Not that I know of," Emma said.

"Couldn't he have done the murder— Oh God, what am I talking about? I shouldn't have said that."

"Go on," Emma said quietly.

"No, of course I didn't mean it. I was just wondering in a theoretical kind of way whether it could have been possible for him to do it as soon as he got into Guy's room at four o'clock."

"I'll ask him in a theoretical kind of way when he comes."

Judith flushed. "No, you mustn't. No, I said I didn't mean it, didn't I? Now you're angry with me. Oh, Lord, why do I always do the wrong thing? Is it living with Sam, d'you think? Have I lost all my normal values? I truly didn't mean it. Please forgive me."

"It doesn't matter," Emma said. "We'll all be thinking some pretty unrealistic things for some time to come, I should imagine, unless they find the murderer quickly."

Judith nodded sombrely and turned to the door. "Let's hope they do."

Emma saw her to the front door, closing it after her as she went out, then returned to the living room, finished her whisky and went to the kitchen, deciding to give Roger up and make some scrambled eggs for her supper.

But she had got only as far as beginning to beat the eggs in a basin when she suddenly put down the fork she was using, left the kitchen, put on her coat and went quickly into the garden. Taking the path round the house, she went down the steps that led to the Hawses' flat. When she rang, rapid footsteps came to the door, it was opened and Mrs. Hawse peered out. A light in the hall fell on her face and Emma thought there was disappointment on it.

"Oh, it's you, Miss Ritchie, I thought most likely it was the police." There would have been more drama about a visit from the police. "They've been questioning Arthur half the afternoon, so he says. Seems he was able to give them a lot of help, being right in the middle of things. What a terrible thing to happen! Who'd have thought it could in a place like King's Weltham?" But she looked as if she had been finding the evening exciting and enjoyable.

"Arthur's home then, is he?" Emma asked.

"Yes, he's just having his supper."

"I'm sorry to interrupt, but could I have a few words with him?"

"Yes, of course, come in." Mrs. Hawse stood aside so that Emma could enter. Raising her voice, she called, "Here's Miss Ritchie wants to speak to you, Arthur."

She took Emma into the living room.

It had been the kitchen before Emma divided the house into flats and was a fair-sized, square room with a modern fireplace filling the cavity where the old cooking range had been. A coal fire glowed pleasantly in it now. The room was very warm and was full of furniture, with an extraordinary quantity of little lace mats distributed over all the polished surfaces. Dark red velvet curtains covered the windows. The television was on and someone was singing about the agonies of love, but Arthur Hawse, seated at the dining table, had his back to it and was eating sausages and chips. When Emma came in he got up and turned the sound down so that it only whispered faintly but left the screen flickering.

"Sit down, Miss Ritchie—have a cup of tea," he offered.

"No, thank you," Emma said. "I've only come for a moment. Please go on with your supper. Don't let it get cold. I just wanted to ask you one question. You saw Dr. Challoner go up to Dr. Lampard's office, didn't you, followed after a moment by Mrs. Fielding—"

"That woman's disappeared, did you know that?" he interrupted, sitting down again and going on with his sausages.

"There's something queer about her that I can't make out. She seemed to know her way about the place, but I've never seen her before."

"If it's true what they're saying about Dr. Lampard and her," Mrs. Hawse said, "perhaps she met him in the evenings, after you'd come home, Arthur."

"Funny place to meet—no comforts to speak of," Arthur Hawse answered sceptically. "I don't believe that story myself."

Emma reminded herself that Arthur hardly ever believed anything, even most obvious things, but for once she was inclined to agree with him.

"Miss Kirby told me she'd gone," she said. "Actually it's Mrs. Fielding I wanted to ask you about. She was quite close behind Dr. Challoner going up the stairs, wasn't she?"

"Well, I reckon she was about at the bottom when he was at the top," he said.

"But he didn't shut the door in her face, did he? When he went into Dr. Lampard's office, he didn't shut the door behind him? It wasn't shut, even for a moment?"

He shook his head. "He got to the door, opened it, then shot into the room, leaving the door wide open behind him, and a moment later Mrs. Fielding got to the door and started screaming." He gave Emma a curious look. "You haven't been worrying yourself that he could have done the murder after going into the room, have you, Miss Ritchie? Because he couldn't have unless the woman saw him do it. And I wouldn't put it past her to lie about it, if she did see it, and maybe try to make some use of it later, but it doesn't fit the facts, as I see them. For one thing, if he'd had murder in his mind, he would have shut the door behind him, wouldn't he? I wouldn't worry."

"I haven't been worrying about that," Emma said. "I know Dr. Challoner. But I did start worrying that there might be something there the police could get hold of. They seem to be keeping him a long time. I was expecting him here some time ago. But what you've told me makes it quite clear that they couldn't work up a suspicion that he'd done the murder then. Anyway, the superintendent seemed to me a very intelligent man, much nicer than I was expecting. I don't think he'll go building up any absurd theories."

"Ah, don't get Walter Day wrong," Arthur said. "I was at school with him. I've known him most of my life. A clever chap, like you said. That's how he's got where he is, while I'm just stuck as a porter. But don't let that manner of his fool you. When he was on the beat he was a terror in a punch-up, and if you was different in your manner to him, you'd soon find he was different to you. You're all nice and quiet-mannered up at the Institute, and you speak posh, so he's nice and quiet-mannered too and he speaks posh to you, but he's tough and ambitious and he's out to catch a murderer. If I was a villain I wouldn't like to come face to face with him."

Emma returned to her flat. She was hoping that Roger might have arrived while she had been absent, but the flat was empty. Wondering if it was possible that he had gone back to his own rooms instead of coming to her, she tried telephoning him there, but there was no answer. She went back to the kitchen and once more started beating the eggs that she had left in the basin, then cut a slice of bread and was just about to slip it in the toaster when the front doorbell rang again.

She knew that it would not be Roger. He would have used his key to let himself in. Hoping that it was not Judith again, because, tired as she was, Emma felt that she had had enough recently of trying to help with the Partletts' problems, she went to the door. With some dismay she found Sam Partlett outside it.

"Mind if I come in for a few minutes?" he asked.

He put a hand against the doorpost to steady himself as he spoke, but Emma did not think that he was drunk. He had a look of almost unbearable fatigue. His face was very white and looked hollow with weariness. His eyes were sunken and his mouth seemed to be dragged to one side in a curious nervous grimace.

She gestured to him to come in. He followed her into the living room.

"Whisky?" she asked, thinking that he looked as if he needed it.

"No, thanks," he said, dropping into a chair before Emma had invited him to sit down. "I've been sitting in the White Hart over one beer for the last hour, trying to make up my mind to come home, but not being able to face it because I knew what Judith was going to say when I did. She'd say that if Guy was murdered he had it coming to him. And if I'd started on whisky I didn't know what I might do. She's never been able to understand that I loved the man."

"So did I," Emma said. "Is that why you've come to see me?"

He nodded. "Yes, I wanted to talk to someone who felt about him as I did. He's meant more to me than anyone else I've ever known—even more, in a way, than Judith, though of course that's something different. I don't have to explain that to you. I've tried to explain it to Judith, but she doesn't understand. She says he's been my evil genius, and perhaps she's right. I've always been a more rational person when I've kept away from him. But he never did you any harm, did he?"

"He did me a great deal of good."

"Ah yes, but you're more stable than I am, and you're a woman too. He wouldn't put the same kind of pressures on you that he did on me. I often hated him for it, then found it was really myself I hated. Take that bungled suicide of mine, for instance, that I was telling you about this afternoon. You see, it was a Sunday and I didn't even know Guy was in the building, and when I came to and found I'd failed I hated him as I never have before or since, because after what I'd done the night before I felt I wasn't fit to live. But then Judith took over and pulled me round, and she's somehow kept me going ever since, though I've often treated her abominably. You've seen something of that. But she just can't understand how much Guy meant to me. She isn't jealous, it isn't anything as simple as that, it's the evil in me that she thinks he brought out. And now she's going to be glad when she hears he's dead, and that's why I've been sitting in the White Hart, trying to put off coming home. Of course, she won't say she's glad, but I'll see it in her eyes." Leaning back, he closed his own eyes. His mouth was still drawn to one side and Emma wondered if it was in an effort to fight off tears. Looking at her again, he went on, "I really came in to ask you if you'd come upstairs with me and help me break the news. It'd cushion things for the moment."

"You needn't worry about breaking the news," Emma said. "She knows about it already. It seems you made her a rather curious telephone call this afternoon and she came down to find out what I thought it meant."

He rubbed his knuckles against his forehead, as if he were trying to collect his thoughts.

"Oh," he said. "That. Yes. It was stupid of me."

"I'm afraid, if you wanted to reassure her, it had the opposite effect," Emma said, "because of course she couldn't understand it at all, and when I told her about Guy's death she leapt to the conclusion you'd been telling her the police suspected you."

He nodded. "Well, I suppose it was what I was doing, though it didn't dawn on me she wouldn't understand me because she didn't know anything about Guy being dead. It was just shock. My mind wasn't working properly. Then someone came into the room—I'd sneaked along to my lab in the confusion after Roger found Guy's body—and I rang off quickly because I didn't want to be overheard."

"Who came in?" Emma asked.

"I'm not sure. I think it was Nixey. But I didn't look round. I just heard someone at the door and slammed the telephone down and joined the others who were going into the common room. But I saw Nixey walking along the passage ahead of me."

"You know the police aren't going to suspect you, don't you?" Emma said.

"Why not?"

"Because I happen to be able to give you a complete alibi."

"Can you? Oh, because I came into your lab and chatted till we went along for tea. I see. But are you sure what time I came in?"

"Pretty sure."

His grimace turned into a kind of smile. "Well, that's very satisfactory. You're always helping us out, Emma. And you don't even like us. But you won't have us on your hands much longer. Without Guy this place will be impossible for me, and Judith never wanted to come here at all."

"Where will you go?"

"I don't know, but we'll go. Go somewhere. You'll soon be rid of us."

"What will you do?"

"I'll think of something. I might even try living on my wife for a little, till I've got all this affair behind me. She's a splendid nurse, you know. I think she could probably get a job quite easily. But one thing I'm sure of is, I'll get out of science. You've seen it—I can't get on with the people and you just can't work by yourself. You're stuck in a community. You can't get away from it. You know, it must have been wonderful long ago when a scientist could work away in the little lab he'd fitted out for himself at the bottom of the garden and didn't have to bother about things like electron microscopes and densitometers and technicians to look after them, and so on. Writers and painters are damned lucky people, the way they can shut the door on the world and just get on with the job, don't you think so?"

"I don't, it wouldn't agree with me at all," Emma said. "I like working with people."

"Well, perhaps it wouldn't really suit me either, but at the moment I feel I know why men become hermits. You can't do much damage to anyone, sitting on top of a pillar or living in a cave in the desert." He stood up. "That's where I'd like to be now, on top of a pillar with nothing but miles and miles of sand all round me. Meanwhile, thank you for letting me talk and for breaking the news to Judith. I don't feel as scared as I did of going up to her. But may I ask you just one thing more?"

"Yes?"

"How can you be so sure about that abili of mine? I couldn't tell you myself what time I came in to see you."

"I happened to look at the clock a few minutes before you came into the room. I know what the time was."

"And the police are sure what time Guy was murdered?"

"Pretty sure."

"I see. Then that's that." His tone had suddenly become ironic. Emma wondered if he knew that her clock and the others in the laboratories along the downstairs passage had gone wrong and was probing to see how much she intended to say about it. "Good night and, again, many thanks."

When he had gone she asked herself why she had not told him about the clocks having been ten minutes slow. Was it simply that she had been very tired and wanted him to leave? That seemed as likely as anything. Returning to the kitchen, she at last succeeded in making her scrambled eggs and coffee and had just finished them when she heard Roger's key in the door.

She went swiftly to meet him, reached out to him and clung to him. He held her tightly. They did not kiss and neither of them spoke. Emma had not realized until she touched him how intensely she had been needing him, but as the sense of his closeness flooded her she became aware of a wonderful feeling of security, a belief that now everything would be all right. It was only momentary, because of course it was nonsense. Roger's presence could not undo what had happened in the afternoon. Yet it seemed to free her from some intolerable tension.

Drawing back from him, she said, "I'll get you something to eat."

"Don't bother," he said. "I've had some sandwiches. But a drink would be welcome."

He took off his overcoat, hung it up in the hall and followed her into the living room. She poured out a whisky for him and took it to him as he sat down by the fire, holding out his hands to its glowing bars.

"Aren't you having one too?" he asked, seeing that she had not poured out a drink for herself.

"I've already had two while I was waiting for you," she said. "I think that's enough for the present."

"I'm sorry I've been such a long time." He was looking very tired, not with the air of emotional exhaustion that had made Sam Partlett's face seem almost unfamiliar, but with the drawn, strained look of someone who has had to carry a load of responsibility that was almost more than he could bear. "I had to go to the police station."

"That's what I thought must have happened," she said as she sat down facing him. "Did they keep you there all this time?"

He nodded.

"But why?"

"For a variety of reasons." He drank some whisky, then sat back in his chair, relaxing. He was silent for a moment, then observed, "It's bloody cold outside. Winter's coming."

"Oh, Roger, please tell me what's been happening," Emma said. "I've been going slightly crazy, waiting for you."

"Yes, all right. It's just that it's rather nice to be quite quiet for a little while. I seem to have been answering questions without stopping for several hours. What have you been doing?"

"Nothing much. Just waiting for you and talking to Judith and Sam and Arthur."

"Judith? Why Judith? Oh, I suppose she wanted to know what had happened."

"Yes, I had to tell her about it. Then I went and asked Arthur a few things. Then Sam came and talked. But I'll come back to that later. Tell me about these questions you've been answering."

"They were mostly about the Institute and the way it's run and were pretty much routine. They wanted to know who was likely to have been where, and when, and why, and whether it was all normal, or whether anyone had done anything strange, and so on. It's all much harder to explain to a member of the lay public, like a policeman, than you'd think, though that man Day is pretty quick. Then they wanted my fingerprints. They're on the razor, of course, and it seems they're the only ones that are. Either the razor was wiped, or the murderer wore gloves. And they gave me to understand that picking up that razor was one of the most foolish actions of my life, which I'm ready to believe it was."

"Why did you do it?" Emma asked.

"I wish I knew. It was just a kind of curiosity, I think, to see if it was one of our standard issue."

"And was it?"

"Oh yes."

"But they aren't suspicious of you, are they?" She felt a shudder of apprehension.

"It's hard to say," he said. "They know I couldn't have done the murder when I went into Guy's room at four o'clock. Luckily for me, I left the door open and walked straight in when I saw him, and that screaming woman was just behind me. But Arthur didn't see me when I went along to the common room. He'd already gone off to have his tea. So I might have gone into Guy's room, say about twenty to four, which is when I think I did actually go along to the common room, and could have gone into his room, cut his throat and gone on to have tea. They've been doing a lot of enquiring about people coming and going in the hall during the time Arthur was away, and it seems there are some gaps when the place could have been empty and I could have done the job."

"But the blood," she said with a tremor in her voice. "Can you cut a person's throat without getting blood onto yourself?"

He gave a crooked smile. "Well, that happens to be awkward." He finished his whisky, stood up and went to get himself a refill. "First of all they wanted to know what I'd done with my lab coat. A lab coat is a very suspicious garment, naturally. It protects one from getting all kinds of stains all over one. They hunted for it in my lab and couldn't find it. So I explained that I never wore a lab coat and haven't owned one for years. They didn't take my word for it, they checked it with Stan, but even when he told them I was speaking the truth they didn't quite believe him. They realized we're good friends and thought he might lie for me. So they checked how long it would have taken me to get to the incinerator with my coat and back again and thought I might just have managed it if I was lucky. And it happens there are some remnants of what might be a lab coat there. Isn't that unfortunate? But it was my picking up that razor that they really couldn't get over." He returned to his chair by the fire. "It gave me such a good reason for having blood on my hands, you see. Of course I might have washed them after doing the murder before going along for my tea, but they seemed to think I was the kind of person who might know that blood doesn't wash off your hands so easily. As a matter of fact, there's some left on them now, though I scrubbed them hard after that scene in Guy's office. They tested them and there's still some round my nails." He put his glass down on a table beside him and held his hands out before him, gazing at them as if he were trying to discern invisible blood.

Emma took her head in her hands, regarding him. "I don't think I really believe any of this."

"As a matter of fact, I'm not sure they do either," he said. "But it's their job to explore every possibility. I was entirely co-operative."

"But your motive," she said. "Isn't it usual to have a motive?"

"They think I've got one. That's another of the kinds of things it's difficult to explain to a layman. They think, because I'm deputy director, that I'll automatically step into Guy's shoes and that that might be why I killed him. I tried to explain that it isn't automatic at all, in fact that it's probable a new director will be brought in from outside. Day nodded politely and said that he understood—that's what he kept saying all the time—but I'm not sure that he did."

"But didn't you tell him that in any case you're going to Adelaide?"

He shook his head. "No."

"Why not?"

"It didn't seem the right time to talk about it."

"I don't see why it shouldn't have been."

"Wouldn't it have sounded a little too convenient? How could he assess how genuinely I wanted to go? And anyway, I'd begun to feel by then that the less I said the better. But actually I wasn't the only one who was doing some talking. Day himself gave me quite a bit of information. That red-haired woman you took care of, she's a phony. The address she gave them in London doesn't exist, and she never registered at the George in Crandwich. She came out of the blue and she's vanished back into it."

"She told me she and Guy had been lovers for years," Emma said, "but that she felt she couldn't leave her husband, who'd been crippled by polio. I felt at the time there was something wrong with the story. I didn't think she was at all Guy's type."

"You don't know what she was like when she was young," Roger replied. "He did stick to people, you know, once he'd started to care for them."

"But she spoke as if there were still an active love affair between them, and she said she'd come here to break it off. I thought there was something odd about that because, if she really had, why did she come to the Institute? Why didn't she meet him more privately in his home or even in her hotel? And she didn't seem to know who Dorothy was. Well, anyone who's known Guy for a little while knows all about Dorothy— Oh, Roger, I've just had an awful thought!"

"What's that?" he asked.

"Dorothy's all alone. I ought to have gone to see her instead of coming straight home. I was only thinking of you and never gave that poor old woman a thought. I wonder what she'll do now."

"Well, it's much too late to go to see her now," Roger said. "She'll have gone to bed long ago. You can drop in on her tomorrow. About the red-haired woman, it's odd that she seemed to know her way about the building. When she arrived she went straight up the stairs to Guy's room without asking Arthur the way, and when she disappeared she must have gone out by the side door beyond the technicians' common room and round the building to the car park, which wouldn't have been an easy way out to find if she didn't know it already. So she must have been here before to meet Guy, whether it was because they were lovers or for some other reason."

"What other reason can you think of?"

"Something she didn't want the police to know about, or why did she give them that false address? Perhaps she came to him for money."

"Are you thinking of blackmail?" she asked incredulously.

"No, I don't think Guy would have fallen for blackmail," he answered. "But he was generous with money, you know. He might simply have been helping her for old times' sake in a way she didn't want her crippled husband to know about."

"Then why did she have to spin a yarn to me and the police

about their being lovers? If that gets round to the crippled husband, it won't exactly cheer him up, will it?"

"It may just have seemed the easiest story to tell to account for her being here. I just don't know, Emma. I've been all over this with the police and got nowhere."

"It wasn't very efficient of them, was it, letting her slip through their fingers?"

"They're aware of the fact. They weren't keeping an eye yet on that side entrance and they didn't check up immediately that she was really staying at the George."

"What have they made of Stan's story of the barbiturates?" she asked.

"Well, that supplies a possible motive for the murder, doesn't it?" he said. "Stan finds out that they've gone missing, tells Guy, Guy says he thinks he knows who's been taking them and he'll deal with it himself, and a few days later someone cuts his throat." He stretched wearily and gave a long-drawn yawn. "God, I'm tired. Incidentally, the police are sure it was done by someone he knew well."

"Why's that?"

"Because Guy was sitting at his desk when we found him, and apparently it's certain that whoever killed him stood behind him to do it. So the way Day thinks it happened is that the murderer came to visit Guy and was roaming about the room, chatting to him while he stayed at his desk, and then got behind him, leant over him and did the job. There are no signs that he struggled. But I've been taking for granted all along that it was one of us who did it, because of that razor. It's one of ours. But whoever used it has probably replaced it already from the store cupboard, so looking to see if one's missing from anyone's lab isn't going to help much."

"Did the police tell you about the clocks?" Emma asked.

"Clocks? No. Why?"

She told him how it had been found that the clocks in the

rooms off the downstairs passage were all slow. He thought about it for a while, frowning, sipping his whisky.

At last he said, "So you think someone tampered with them."

She spread her hands out. "If they didn't, it's just a queer co-incidence. A very queer one though. But what I can't see is who would gain by changing them. The first person I thought of was Sam. But he'd actually lose by doing it. If my clock was right, and I think it was, when I got in from Crandwich in the afternoon, I can give him a perfect alibi. He came into my lab only a few minutes after I got in to apologize for having walked out on my party. He told me he'd lost his temper with Bill and walked out before he felt tempted to make a scene. And he went to see Guy to tell him he was going to leave King's Weltham, but Guy gave him a few drinks and persuaded him to stay, then drove him home, and there was that bit of trouble between him and Judith that we overheard, but either he got himself under control or she did it for him. Anyway, he stayed on with me till we went along together to the common room and Arthur was back in his office by then and would have seen us go by. But you see, if my clock was slow when Sam came to see me, the time wasn't twenty-five past three, as I thought, it was really twenty-five to four, and he might just have had time to slip up to Guy's room after Arthur went to have tea, do the murder and come to see me. It would have been a tight fit even then, but he could just have done it, though I don't know what he'd have done about bloodstains. Still, it might have been possible."

Roger nodded, again giving the matter some thought before he went on. "So Sam wasn't the one who tampered with the clocks. Who else is there? Who stands to benefit?"

"I've been thinking about that," she answered, "but I can't see that anyone does. It looks as if it must have been someone with a room down that passage, yet neither Bill nor Ernest would gain anything by it. They both went along to the common room while Arthur was away, so either of them could have slipped into Guy's room without Arthur seeing them. But what would have been the point of changing the clocks? It wouldn't have given either of them an alibi. No, the only possibility I can think of, and I don't like to think about it, is that it was done to incriminate Sam."

"You're thinking of Bill."

She shied away from the explicit statement. "It might have been anyone who'd happened to see Sam come into my lab at twenty-five past three and thought he could muddle things up."

"But whoever he was, when did he get along the passage to change the clocks?" Roger asked.

"I know of two people who went along the passage while we were still milling about in the hall after you'd discovered Guy's body. One was Sam. He told me himself this evening that he went straight to his lab to telephone Judith, but he didn't finish the call because he realized there was someone at the door who could hear what he was saying, and he's almost certain it was Ernest."

"Ernest! My God, it isn't thinkable that he'd either murder Guy or try to incriminate Sam."

"But we've just agreed it couldn't have been Sam himself."

"Yes." He stroked the side of his chin. "That telephone call—why should he have minded if Ernest overheard him if he was simply telling Judith about the murder?"

"He seems to have been in the middle of telling her not to worry, that the police didn't suspect him, as if he thought she'd take for granted they would. He says now he knows he wasn't being rational, and stopping in the middle, as he did, all he managed to do was drive her crazy with worry."

"We may be able to check on that call. One of the switchboard girls may have listened in. We'll at least be able to check the time of it. How much of this have you told the police?"

"About the telephone call and Ernest overhearing it, nothing at all. I only heard it from Judith and Sam after I'd got home."

"I think you ought to tell them."

"But not tonight! For heaven's sake, not tonight!" She desperately wanted Roger to herself for the rest of the evening. "It can wait till tomorrow, can't it?"

"I think Day was expecting to be working most of the night," Roger said. "He's still got a lot of people lined up for questioning."

"Then let him get on with it. I think we've both had all we can take for the moment. You didn't feel it was the right time to tell them about Adelaide. I don't feel it's the right time to do any more talking."

"Adelaide," Roger said, and looked as if his thoughts had gone far away, perhaps as far as the other side of the world. "Of course, I shouldn't really have gone."

"What d'you mean?" Emma said. "You'd an appointment with Guy to tell him you were resigning."

"But when it came to the point I shouldn't have done it. You wouldn't have come with me and in the end that's all that matters."

"But I would have come. I will come. It's what you want, isn't it?"

"Is it? I hardly know any more. We've been over it too often."

"I'm sure you want to go. You've been here much too long. You need a change. And I'll come. I've quite made up my mind about it."

He gave her a sardonic look, an oddly unkind one. "Because there's nothing to keep you here any longer?"

She understood him, yet could not quite believe in it. "I don't know what you mean."

"Well, Guy's gone now," he said. "You've got to let go of him, whether you want to or not. So at last you're ready to come with me."

"Guy's death has nothing to do with it. You know that."

"Do I? I think it's got a good deal to do with it."

"You're absolutely wrong. As a matter of fact, I'd made up my mind about it before the time of your appointment with Guy. I was having a hairdo and I was under the dryer when I suddenly saw clearly what I wanted to do. And I was glad I was having my hair done, because I thought that if I was going to be accepting a proposal of marriage it was just as well to be looking my best."

"In that case, why didn't you say something about it before I went up to see Guy?"

She could tell that he did not believe her. "First, because Sam came to see me and kept me talking. Then as soon as I got into the common room Maureen got hold of me. And anyway, the room was full of people. It wouldn't have been easy to talk about something as important as that."

"If it was as important as that to you, you could have got rid of Sam. You could have brushed Maureen off. You could have said something to me."

She said in an astonished tone, "We're quarrelling."

"Don't let it bother you. Most people do it sooner or later," he said. "Perhaps it would have been good for us to do it much sooner." He stood up, preparing to leave. "I couldn't bear it, you know, if you only came with me because you'd lost Guy. I've always realized that in the ways that count he was more important to you than I was and his death somehow makes that worse. Death brings things to the surface, doesn't it? I don't want to take you on as a kind of widow."

"But, Roger, none of that is true."

"There's much more truth in it than you've ever faced."

"If that's how you feel, I think you should go to Adelaide without me."

She stood up facing him. Both their faces were pale, but on both of them, making them look oddly alike, there was a bright flush along the cheekbones.

"That may be the answer," he said, and turned to the door.

She did not move as she heard him put on his coat in the hall, open the front door, go out and close it behind him.

CHAPTER 7

Emma did not expect to sleep, yet when she went to bed she slept as deeply as if she had been drugged. When she woke at about half past seven the next morning her mind was a blank. There was no trace in it of anything that had happened the day before, but only a shadowy emptiness, filled with an unreasoning sense of fear. Then she remembered her quarrel with Roger.

Compared with the quarrels that went on in the flat overhead, it had been a very small, very civilized quarrel, yet it might in its way be as disastrous as any of those. But there was something else besides the quarrel that she ought to remember. Burying her face in the pillow, becoming aware that she was still only half conscious, she suddenly remembered Guy's murder and was shocked wide awake.

Getting up, she put on her dressing gown and went to the kitchen to make coffee. She had remembered what she intended to do that morning. She was going to see Dorothy. Yet it was nearly ten o'clock before she set out. She was filled with a dreary lethargy, a deep unwillingness to face the day ahead. The events of yesterday had begun to have a meaning for her that she had not faced till now. She began to understand what it would mean to her that she would never see Guy again, that she would never again meet the small grey eyes that could change in their expression so rapidly from the utmost kindliness to a malicious sort of intelligence, or to a blankness that put up an impassable barrier between her and him. She recognized that she had never known what kind of man he really was and that now she never would.

The person who probably knew more about him than anyone else was Dorothy, but even if she was ready to confide in Emma, which was unlikely, she was an inarticulate old woman who probably would not be able to put her knowledge into words. But she must be feeling lost and alone. It was only normal kindness to call on her. Yet Mrs. Hawse had arrived and was using the vacuum cleaner in the living room by the time Emma felt up to going out to the garage, backing her car out of it and driving towards the Institute.

The drive to the director's house branched off the main drive a hundred yards or so before it reached the big building. She saw police cars outside the main entrance. But there were none outside Guy's house. Yet as she stopped her car near the door and got out, it seemed to her that the place had a desolate quiet. This must be imagination, she thought, until she realized that the curtains at all the windows were drawn. It made the house look blind and deserted. Dorothy, of course, belonged to a generation that greeted death with drawn curtains and probably deep mourning. Emma went to the door and rang the bell.

After the sound of it had died away she waited patiently, knowing that even if the old woman had heard the bell it would take her some time to reach the door. Presently Emma heard the sound of slow footsteps inside and the door was opened.

Dorothy, as she had expected, was in black. But when she came to think of it, Emma remembered that Dorothy had always worn black, a much-darned lamb's-wool twin set, a badly seated skirt with a drooping hemline, wrinkled black stockings and surprisingly heavy shoes, which she wore inside the house as well as out of it. Her face was a complicated pattern of crisscross lines, with skin that seemed to have almost nothing between it and the hard bone behind it. She had pale eyes behind thick, steel-rimmed spectacles. They had always an oddly questioning look, as if she were constantly trying to understand something that was just beyond her. Her age was somewhere between eighty and ninety.

In all the years that Emma had known her, she had never seemed to alter, any more than the twin set and sagging skirt had ever seemed to be replaced by new ones. Emma knew that Guy had made several attempts to induce the old woman to dress a little more cheerfully, buying her pretty silk blouses and light-coloured cardigans, chosen with Emma's help, but Emma sometimes wondered if Dorothy had ever even taken them out of their wrappings. In some drawer in one of the upstairs rooms there must be a pile of them as untouched as when they were bought. It was impossible, but it seemed to Emma that the very darns in the succession of black cardigans that Dorothy must have worn out during the time they had known one another were always in the same places.

"Oh, it's you, Miss Ritchie," Dorothy said without any sign of interest, though as usual the questioning look was there in her eyes, as if she were wondering if Emma had brought her more bad news. "Come in. They've only just been here, asking me all about you."

"You mean the police?" Emma said.

"That's right." The old woman's tone implied that she could not have meant anything else. " 'There's nothing much I can tell you,' I said, 'I've got better things to do than listen to gossip,' but that's the way they are, asking you the same thing over and over again. I said to them, I said, 'I know my memory isn't what it was, but I'm sure you asked me that only five minutes ago and I told you I didn't know anything.' Would you like a cup of tea?"

"No, thank you," Emma said as she advanced into the small square hall, made murky by the closely drawn curtains. "I just called in to see if you're all right."

"I don't know what you call all right," Dorothy said, preceding Emma into the sitting room, where the light was as dim as in the hall. "I suppose I'm as all right as can be expected in the circumstances. I can't get over it yet that he's gone before me. A young man like him, I thought he'd live thirty years longer than me. 'What will you do when I die?' I used to say to him. 'You ought to marry,' I said, 'and have a wife to take care of you. Why don't you marry that Miss Ritchie?' I said. 'She'd have you tomorrow, she doesn't really care for that Dr. Challoner, she's only taken up with him because you don't speak up.' You don't mind me speaking my mind, do you? I know I'm only speaking the truth and it's too late now to make any difference."

They sat down in the twilit room, which was strangely stripped of Guy's presence already. Dorothy must have been round it this morning, tidying up, for there were no books or papers lying about and even in the dimness Emma could see a gleam of polish on the light-coloured, modern furniture.

"Did you say all those things to the police?" Emma asked.

"I always speak my mind," Dorothy said. Her back was very bent and she looked very small and hunched in her large chair. "It's a way you get into when you're as old as I am. You stop minding what people think of you."

"But did you tell them that I wanted to marry Dr. Lampard?"

"I may have."

"Don't you remember?"

"Not exactly. I told you my memory isn't what it was."

"But you also said you could remember what they'd asked you five minutes before."

"And so I can."

"So you can remember what you told them about Dr. Lampard and me."

"Well, what does it matter?" the old woman said indifferently. "They'd have found out all about it anyway from somebody else."

Emma had a feeling that it might matter very much.

"You know it isn't true, don't you?" she said.

"Well, if it isn't, it isn't, but I've got eyes in my head," Dorothy replied.

With her own eyes becoming accustomed to the semi-darkness, Emma could see the look in Dorothy's sunken eyes as she spoke, a look that disconcertingly was almost mirthful, and with a shock Emma realized that the old woman did not like her and had probably enjoyed gossiping about her to the police, possibly knowing quite well that what she said was untrue.

It had never occurred to Emma before to wonder whether or not Dorothy liked her. She had always taken her for granted, without thinking about her feelings. She had always been there, she had been simply one of the facts of life. But if what Dorothy had always felt for Guy throughout the years had been a strong and deep possessiveness, his attachment to Emma, long-lasting too, could have filled her with bitter jealousy. And even if she had understood perfectly well how little there had been of the truly sexual about it, it would only have been in sexual terms that she would have been able to describe it to the police. The sort of dependence that Emma and Guy had had on one another would have been too complex a thing for her to convey, even if intuitively she had understood it.

But why had the police questioned her about it? That disturbed Emma a good deal.

"What will you do now?" she asked. "Where will you go?"

"I'll be all right," Dorothy answered. "He said I would be. He said it was in his will. He said he'd put aside enough to take care of me for the rest of my days. I don't know how he left the rest of it. He didn't talk about that kind of thing. What he told me was just to set my mind at rest. 'If I die,' he said, 'you'll hear from Hubbard and Hubbard of Lincoln's Inn, you've nothing to worry about.' But who'd have thought he'd go before me, a young man like him?" To Dorothy, Guy's middle age was still youth. "I told him so," she said, "but he told me people ought to make wills, that if they didn't it was because they were afraid, or selfish or something. Not that he wasn't selfish about other things. He could drive me mad sometimes, asking for this and for that. A wife wouldn't have done for him all that I used to do."

Emma thought that Guy might not have done for a wife as much as he had been in the habit of doing for Dorothy.

"Have you any relations or friends to go to?" she asked.

"I haven't thought about it yet," Dorothy said. "I've relations, but we've never seen much of one another. I wouldn't be welcome. And I've never bothered much with friends. I had all I needed, living here. All I want now is just a room where I can be comfortable. I believe there are old people's homes that are really very nice if you can afford a good one. But I can take my time thinking about it. I know there's money, that's the main thing."

Emma stood up. "Well, let me know if I can help in any way."

"Thank you, Miss Ritchie, you're very kind."

But Dorothy did not like her, however kind she said Emma was. Emma could read it in the faintly malicious glint in the pale eyes behind the thick spectacles. She could put real effort into being kind to Dorothy, could look for one of those nice old people's homes for her, could make a habit of visiting her there, but still Dorothy would not like her. And now that she realized that, Emma also realized that she did not like Dorothy and never had, that she had always thought her a selfish old person who after her fashion had exploited Guy quite cleverly.

"I'm glad he took care of you," she said. "I'm going along to my lab now. Don't get up. Good-bye."

She went quickly to the door, but she paused there.

"I meant to ask you, Dorothy," she said, "do you know a Mrs. Fielding?"

Dorothy shook her head.

"A very thin woman, middle-aged, with bright red hair," Emma said.

Dorothy shook her head again.

"She wasn't a friend of Dr. Lampard's, that you know of?"

"He didn't go for the type that dyes their hair," Dorothy said decidedly, "which is what it would be if she's middle-aged."

"You've never seen her? She's never been here?"

"No."

"Oh well . . ." It was what Emma had expected. Letting herself out of the house, glad to emerge from its sombre dusk even into the grey daylight of the November morning, she drove to the car park, left her car there and went in at the main entrance of the Institute.

One police car was still parked outside it. As she went in Arthur Hawse greeted her and told her that Sir Peter Walsh, secretary of the research council that controlled the affairs of King's Weltham, had arrived and at present was in the library with Dr. Challoner and most of the rest of the staff. Emma supposed that she ought to join them and went up to the library.

Sir Peter, whom she had met on a few formal occasions, was in the midst of saying that for the present Dr. Challoner would of course be in charge of the Institute, but that it was too soon, after the tragedy of the day before, to consider the question of replacing Dr. Lampard, who was, need it be said, irreplaceable. As soon as the meeting broke up Emma left the room and went to her laboratory.

She did not delude herself that there was any point in trying to work on her paper, or even to tackle some merely mechanical chores, such as sugar determinations for background information. Sitting down in the chair at her desk, she looked out over the roofs of the greenhouses at the leaden sky where heavy clouds, dingy as huge heaps of dirty washing waiting to be sent to the laundry were piling up. There would be rain later, she thought. Meanwhile she wished that she could go to see Roger and straighten out the stupid quarrel of the evening before. But he would probably have Sir Peter on his hands for the rest of the morning, if not for the rest of the day, and the fact was not to be escaped that while she had been at the meeting in the library he had been careful not to meet her eyes.

She sat thinking of Dorothy and of her dislike and of her belief that Emma had been in love with Guy and she began to wonder if all this time she had been blind to a much fiercer jealousy in Roger than she had ever dreamt that he could feel. Even now she could not bring herself to believe in it. Sitting there, gazing out of the window, she heard the door open and turned her head quickly, hoping that it was Roger, but it was Ernest Nixey.

His face had the grey, papery look of someone who has not slept. He seemed even more shrunken inside his clothes than he usually did. His large brown eyes seemed magnified by distress. It appeared to Emma that he was taking Guy's death very hard, which did not surprise her, because she knew that Ernest was a highly emotional man who would always be appalled by the thought of death, no matter whose. Yet there was an air of desperation about him that was more than she would have expected.

"Am I interrupting you?" he asked, advancing cautiously a little way into the room.

"Not in the least," she said. "I'm doing nothing."

"There are all sorts of things I ought to be doing," he said. "With Mollie away, letters have been piling up feet deep on my desk, and I suppose I could borrow Maureen now to help me get on with them, but I've got a kind of cloud in my mind that comes down and blots out everything as soon as I try to think. D'you ever feel like that, Emma—that your brain's turning into a kind of grey soup that's going to slop over everything at any moment? D'you think it means I'm going mad?"

"I think what it means is that for a long time you've had too much worry for anyone to bear and that somehow you'll have to take a rest," Emma said. "Would you like some of my beastly instant coffee?"

"I should, I should very much." He climbed onto one of the stools. "But I can't take a rest, you know. It's absolutely out of the question."

She filled the kettle, plugged it in and got clean cups out of the cupboard.

"If it's true what you say, that your wife doesn't even know you when you go to see her," she said, spooning coffee into the cups, "I don't see why you shouldn't take a holiday. It wouldn't be disloyal to her. That's what you're afraid of, isn't it? Go to the Canaries or Madeira—anywhere there's sunshine. I'm sure it would help you."

"There'd be chaos here if I did, you know, now of all times," he said. "I couldn't think of it."

"Let there be chaos. There'd be nothing you couldn't sort out when you came back, feeling fit and fine."

He gave her a sad smile. "I know you mean well, Emma, but these things cost money. Oh, God, money! It was bad enough before, but now—I just don't know—I can't think—it's all quite impossible. The nightmare's got too much for me. I don't know what to do."

The kettle began to hum. She turned to it, wishing that she knew whether or not to show how deeply she felt concerned for him, whether open sympathy would not only make him lose what control of himself he had left. She did not understand what was wrong with him, but it was as if Guy's death had affected him even more shatteringly than it had herself, and that was strange, for she was sure that she had been fonder of Guy than Ernest ever had.

"Here's your coffee," she said, taking a cup to him.

There was something blind about the way he looked at her as he took it.

"I don't know what to do," he muttered again.

"About your wife?" she asked. "About your job? About Guy's death? What is it, Ernest?"

He did not answer, but sipped the hot coffee with a deepening frown on his face.

"There isn't anything you know about it, is there?" she said. "Something you haven't told anyone?"

"Oh, for God's sake!" Looking furious, he gulped some coffee and spluttered at the heat of it.

"I'm sorry, I didn't mean to upset you," she said.

"I'm not upset," he declared unconvincingly.

"I was just wondering why you came along this passage after Roger discovered Guy's body. You did, didn't you?"

"Yes, I did, I don't know why, except that I just automatically came to my room. It seemed the normal place to go to. Then I realized that Roger had asked us all to go to the common room to wait for the police, so I went along there."

"Did you see Sam in his lab when you came along the passage?"

"Let me think. Yes, I believe I did. Yes, his door was open and he was at the telephone." Ernest had calmed down somewhat. "Why, is that important?"

"I don't know. I don't know what's important. You didn't see anyone else, did you?"

"I believe there was someone in Bill's room. I suppose it was Bill. Why, Emma? What does it matter where any of us was *after* Guy's murder?"

"It's just that something rather funny happened about the clocks in the rooms along this passage, either in the afternoon before Guy's death or just after it. Not in your room, I believe, but haven't you noticed that the one in Mollie's room is ten minutes slow? Or has it been put right again?"

"I don't know. It's slow, is it? I hadn't noticed." He looked at his watch, then up at Emma's clock. "Yes, I see what you mean. Shall I put it right for you?"

"I'm waiting for the police to put it right. I don't think we should touch it. And if I were you, I think I'd leave Mollie's as it is."

"You think it's got something to do with the murder?"

"It might have something to do with somebody's alibi."

Ernest thought about it for a moment, then shook his head. "Not with mine. I haven't one. But I haven't a motive either. If there's anyone to whom Guy's death is an utter disaster—apart, I mean, from the plain horror of it—but he always said I wasn't to talk about it, though now that he's dead—no, I mustn't think about that. I simply don't know what to do, that's the trouble. I'm in a terrible position. But I've got to keep going somehow, I can't afford to break down. Have you ever wanted to have a breakdown, Emma? I can't help feeling that to have one, a really complete one, would be a wonderful luxury. No one could expect anything of one. No, I'm sorry—" He finished his coffee hastily and put his cup down. "I'm talking nonsense. I didn't come to burden you with my troubles, I just wanted a chat, because I don't seem able to get ahead with any work. I'll think about those clocks, though they don't mean anything to me at the moment."

He darted out of the room.

Emma sat where she was for a little while, thinking that there was only one thing that she wanted just then and that was to go and find Roger and make peace with him. The more she heard of other people's problems, the more she wanted to solve her own. The chances were that he was feeling the same, but one of them would have to make the first move. And for the present he was tied up with Sir Peter. But perhaps she could somehow have a few minutes alone with him. She got up and started towards the door.

At just that moment it opened again. She was sure that this

time it was Roger and was ready to go into his arms without one word of explanation about the quarrel, which suddenly seemed as if it had happened a long time ago and was of no importance, but she recoiled abruptly, for it was Superintendent Day who came in.

Emma remembered what Arthur Hawse had said of the superintendent: that when he had been on the beat he had been a terror in a punch-up and that a real crook would not find him as pleasant and as easy to talk to as she had, but looking at the gangling figure in the shabby suit and at his sad, down-curving smile, she found it difficult to believe that he could be menacing.

"Could you spare me a cup of coffee, I wonder?" he said. "I smelt it as I came along the passage. It's several hours since I had breakfast."

Emma turned to the cupboard where she kept her cups.

"Is it true that Mrs. Fielding's vanished?" she asked.

"I'm afraid so," he said. "Letting her get away like that is one of the sillier mistakes I've made in my time."

"And you don't know who she is?"

He hesitated. "No, but *what* she is—well, we've certain ideas. You brought her in here, didn't you, then left her with Miss Kirby?"

"Yes," Emma said. "She seemed to be in a state of collapse. I thought she was going to have hysterics. So I brought her in here and made her some coffee. Then when you wanted me I got Miss Kirby to look after her and by the time I came down again she'd gone." She plugged the kettle in once more and made coffee for the superintendent and a second cup for herself.

He watched her while she was doing it, then as she handed his cup to him said, "That collapse of hers, did you think it was genuine, or did you think it might have been a dodge for getting away from all the people in the common room?"

138

Emma returned to the chair at her desk. "I did have some doubts about it."

"Why?" He sat on one of the stools.

"I think it was just that I'd known Dr. Lampard pretty well for a long time, but I'd never met her or heard him speak of her. Yet he wasn't specially reticent about such things. I generally knew about it when he was having an affair with a woman."

"Did you mind that?" He looked at Emma with a sort of solicitude, which made her think once more of a doctor, probing an injury to see how much it hurt.

"No," she said. "Why should I?"

"I had an impression—I somehow got the idea"—he was tentative—"that Dr. Lampard meant a great deal to you."

"He did."

"Then didn't these affairs distress you?"

She smiled. "It sounds as if you've been listening to Dorothy. She has an idea I was in love with Dr. Lampard. Actually, I'm engaged to be married to Dr. Challoner." But was she, she wondered suddenly, or was that no longer true? Falling back on what was certainly true, she added, "It's fairly well known that he and I have been having what you call an affair for a long time."

He nodded in a way that showed that he had heard this.

"I've talked to Mrs. Hawse as well as Dorothy," he said. "Two very fluent women. And they both believe the reason you haven't married Dr. Challoner is that you hoped to marry Dr. Lampard."

"I'm afraid they've misled you," Emma said. "But may I ask why any of this is of interest to you?"

"Well, if those two women can think as they do," he said, "isn't it possible that there are other people who do too?"

She looked at him blankly for a moment, then all at once realized what it was, in a roundabout way, that he was saying. It surprised her that she did not feel angrier about it, then she recognized that one of the reasons why she did not was simply that what she felt far more strongly than anger was fear. And with the recognition of her fear came the feeling that she must remain very calm, very quiet.

"You're talking of Dr. Challoner, of course," she said. "You're suggesting that he may have been jealous of Dr. Lampard and that that could have given him a motive for the murder."

"You're very direct." There was a momentary gleam of approval in his eyes. "I was doing my best to approach the matter tactfully."

"I think I prefer directness."

"Very well then, to put the question directly, mightn't Dr. Challoner have had a motive? And he had time to do it, you know, and there's that unfortunate business of getting blood on his hands. That could have been deliberate. And there are one or two other things . . ."

Emma waited for him to go on. She was getting used to her fear now, beginning to feel that she had it under control.

But what he said next took her by surprise. "Has it occurred to you that Mrs. Fielding may not have been going to see Dr. Lampard?"

"But didn't she tell you herself that she was going to see him?" she said.

"Oh, as to what she told us . . ." He shrugged his shoulders. "But just think what we actually know about her. She came in at the main entrance at just about the time Dr. Challoner started up the stairs to go to Dr. Lampard's room. That room is on a half landing, in full view of Hawse's office. He saw her come in and go up the stairs after Dr. Challoner. Then Dr. Challoner opened Dr. Lampard's door and went in, leaving it open. She saw into the room and stood still and started screaming. But suppose Dr. Challoner hadn't left the door open but had shut it in her face and she hadn't seen in. There are stairs going off right and left from that half landing. The ones to the right lead to

Miss Kirby's office, the library and Dr. Challoner's laboratory. The ones to the left lead to a landing with toilets off it and another staircase that leads to the laboratories on the top floor. A number of people came down from that upper floor to the common room about three-thirty and several of them happen to have come down in a group, which gives them all alibis. There are one or two who claim not to have come downstairs at all and we're checking those as carefully as we can to see if any of them has a record of abnormality or violence or any apparent motive for the murder, but most of them up there seem to be junior people, appointed fairly recently, and we haven't got anywhere with them. I'm still interested, however, in the possibility that Mrs. Fielding, if that's her name, which it probably isn't, had no intention of going to Dr. Lampard's room and wouldn't have stopped on that half landing at all if she hadn't seen into the room, but would have gone straight upstairs, either to the right or the left, to meet someone else. What do you think about that?"

For the first time, behind the amiability, Emma sensed the hardness of which Arthur Hawse had told her, but meeting Day's steady gaze, hers was as calm as his.

"Not much," she said. "If she was going to visit Dr. Challoner, which I suppose is what you're talking about, why didn't she call out to him when she saw him on the stairs ahead of her?"

"Perhaps she didn't want to draw Hawse's attention to the fact that she was going to visit him."

Emma shook her head. "You'll be wasting your time if you pursue that line of enquiry."

"But she came here to see someone, and you yourself are doubtful if it was Dr. Lampard."

"The building's crawling with people. It could have been anyone." She looked up at the clock on the wall. "About those clocks," she said, "hasn't it struck you that the one person who definitely couldn't have tampered with them was Dr. Challoner? We all saw him come out of Dr. Lampard's room, then go to his own room to wash the blood off his hands, and then he came to the common room. I suppose it's just conceivable that he might have come along this passage after washing his hands and before going to the common room, but don't you think Hawse would have seen him? He's a person whom Hawse would have noticed, you know. So you see, he couldn't have done it."

He gave his mild, melancholy smile. "I think you're right, Dr. Ritchie, he couldn't have tampered with the clocks. But it isn't certain that the person who did that is the person who did the murder. The only reason for changing the clocks that we've been able to come up with is that someone wanted to incriminate Dr. Partlett. He's the only person whose alibi it affects. But someone who didn't like him who had nothing to do with the murder may have seized the chance to do that. You understand that, don't you?"

He looked sorry for her as he said it, as if he were just telling her that she might have to undergo a painful operation.

Her anger began to mount. "Oh yes, I understand that you're still trying to pin the murder on Dr. Challoner. For some reason you like that solution. You think the altering of the clocks is a relatively minor matter. But do you know that at least three people came along this passage during the time I'm speaking about, before we all went to the common room, and any of them could have changed the clocks?"

His eyebrows went up. "No. I didn't know that."

"Well, talk to Dr. Nixey then. He came along here and he heard Dr. Partlett talking on his telephone. It was a call to his wife. She told me about it. And Mr. Nixey saw someone in Dr. Carver's room who he thinks was Dr. Carver."

"That's very interesting," Day said slowly, "though it doesn't affect what I said, that the object of changing the clocks was only an attempt to incriminate Dr. Partlett. Can you think of any other reason for it?"

"It might have been an attempt to incriminate me."

"Yes, that's possible. So there we are. Now there's one more thing I wanted to ask you." He finished his coffee and put his cup down. "In layman's terms, can you tell me what a buffer solution is? I've asked Dr. Challoner about it, but I'm afraid what he told me went over my head."

"That's a bit difficult," she said. "It's a solution that stabilizes acidity."

"The acidity of what?"

"Well, of an experimental system."

"Um. I see. I don't think I'll get far trying to understand you either. But you need barbiturates for it?"

"You can use barbiturates. Some people still do, though it's a bit old-fashioned. There are other things you can use."

"But someone here's been using barbiturates. That's normal, is it?"

"Oh yes."

"And you know they've been disappearing?"

"So Mr. Rankin told me."

He looked thoughtful, then stood up.

"I told you we didn't know anything for certain about Mrs. Fielding," he said, "but it struck me, you see, when I was talking to her, that she'd some of the symptoms of a drug addict, and when we knew barbiturates came into the picture, it seemed probable that someone here had been supplying her. Strange, though, how no one here seems ever to have seen her and yet how she knew her way about the building. She knew where she wanted to go when she came into it and she knew how to slip out of it by that side entrance. Have you any ideas about that, Dr. Ritchie?"

Suddenly she wanted to laugh at him. "Oh, it's obvious, isn't it? If you're right that it was Dr. Challoner that she was coming to see, then he must have been the person who was stealing the drugs and no doubt selling them to her at great profit. But then Dr. Lampard found it out, so he had to be killed, and actually Mrs. Fielding saw Dr. Challoner do it, having come up the stairs just behind him by arrangement, so as to be able to swear he couldn't have done it, and then, at a signal from him, she started screaming. It's all very neat and immensely convincing."

His melancholy face was more sombre than usual. "I wish I could be as sure as you are that it's a joke. In my job one can't afford many jokes. But how careless of Dr. Challoner it is to have so many possible motives for murdering Dr. Lampard. There's ambition. I know he says it isn't certain that he'll step into Dr. Lampard's shoes, but it's possible, isn't it? Then there's jealousy. You say there's nothing in that, but he mightn't have been so sure of it. And then there's greed. Drugs fetch a good price on the black market. However, I've kept you long enough. Thank you for being so patient and for the coffee."

He left the room.

For a little while Emma sat where she was, wondering why she had the feeling that he had said something important that had had nothing to do with his suspicions of Roger. Then the door opened again and this time, at last, it was Roger.

"I was wondering if you'd like to come into Crandwich for lunch," he said.

There was no sign on his face or in his voice that he remembered that they had parted the evening before after one of the first real quarrels of their relationship. Emma was sure that he remembered it as clearly as she did but that he had decided that the best thing to do about it was to bury it quietly without an inquest. She was glad of it.

"Haven't you got to take Walsh out to lunch?" she said.

"He's gone already," he answered. "Bill took him to the station. Bill was very eager to make a personal contact with him and that suited me. How about coming into Crandwich?"

She stood up. "Yes, let's go." She took her coat off its peg and slipped it on. "I've just had a long session with the superintendent. He told me that that woman, Mrs. Fielding, is probably a drug addict and probably mixed up in the theft of the barbiturates. Has he told you about that?"

"Yes," he said, "and I've started wondering . . ." He stopped as he opened the door and they started along the passage. But as they went out through the main entrance and set off towards the car park, he went on, "The fact is, if someone's been stealing the stuff and selling it, they may have been making quite a sizeable sum of money, and who's given signs recently of having more money than it's easy to account for? Well, the answer's obvious, isn't it? How has Ernest been managing to keep his wife in a place like Manstead House? He could hardly do that on his salary."

CHAPTER 8

After that neither of them wanted to speak for some time. They set off in Roger's car and were almost in Crandwich before Emma said, "Have you said anything about Ernest to the police?"

"No," Roger said. "They'll get around to it themselves if there's anything in it."

"What do you think barbiturates are worth on the black market?" she asked.

"I haven't any idea."

"Nothing like cannabis or heroin, are they?"

"I shouldn't think so."

"And the amount that's been vanishing can't be very great, or Stan would have noticed it sooner."

He nodded.

"So whoever has been taking the stuff," Emma said, "probably hasn't been getting more than pocket money out of it."

"Not nearly enough to keep a wife in Manstead House, that's what you mean."

"Yes."

"I hope you're right." He turned the car into the car park of the George. "But it's a problem where Ernest has been getting the money from, isn't it?"

"He may have private means that he's never talked about," Emma said. "Most people feel it's bad manners to talk about how much money they've got. And he's an accountant. He may have been clever about investing what he has."

They both got out of the car and Roger locked it.

Walking towards the entrance to the hotel, he said, "Perhaps • he was clever investing what he made from the barbiturates."

"You don't really believe that."

"Why not?"

"Because he's—oh, he's much too nice to be involved in a thing like a drug racket."

"You think, because he's so loyal to that mad wife of his, he's incapable of anything as nasty as that. Yet it might be just that loyalty that could drive him to theft."

"But we aren't talking just about theft, are we?" Emma said. "We're talking about murder."

They went into the small dark entrance hall of the George, which was an old building with low ceilings and plentiful black beams in its walls.

"Not necessarily," Roger said. "We don't know that the drugs and the murder had anything to do with one another. My own belief is that they haven't. I've a theory . . ." But he paused as they went into the bar. "What d'you want? Whisky? Gin?"

Emma asked for a gin and tonic and Roger ordered the same for himself.

The bar was warm and comfortable and seldom very crowded. Today there were only three or four other people there. But unfortunately the barman knew Roger and Emma, who generally came there for a drink and a meal once in every week or two, and naturally he knew of the murder in King's Weltham. Serving them, he dropped his voice confidentially to ask them if it was true that there had already been an arrest.

Roger replied that he had not heard of it.

In a hissing whisper which somehow carried all over the room, so that heads turned and Roger and Emma found themselves the objects of curious glances, the barman said that that fellow Day was a crafty one and the story was that some woman was helping the police with their enquiries. He would have gone on if Roger and Emma had not taken their drinks away from the bar to a settle under a window in one of the thick old walls.

"You said you had a theory," Emma said as they sat down.

Roger shook his head. "Not really. Anyway, it isn't what we came here to talk about, is it? What I wanted to tell you was that I didn't mean what I said last night about you and Guy, or if I did—well, I was a fool."

"I don't think I want to talk about that," Emma said. "Neither of us was normal. But don't let's quarrel again. I can't bear it."

"If we're going to get married, perhaps you'd better get used to it," he said with a smile. "It seems to be a thing that married people do."

"If you're thinking of the Partletts—"

"Damn the Partletts!" he interrupted. "I don't see any reason for you and me to resemble them in any way. But we are going to get married, aren't we?"

"Oh yes."

"Then after lunch I think we ought to go and buy you a ring. Later, if you like, we can go to London and get you something in diamonds, but I want to get you something today. It'll only be something small, as it'll have to come from that antique shop in the square, and you needn't wear it if you feel this isn't the right time to show it off, but I want you to come with me and choose it this afternoon."

"I'm not specially fond of diamonds," she said, her voice a little shaky.

"And we won't go to Adelaide."

"But I want to go to Adelaide."

"No, we'll settle in King's Weltham. If you want to, we'll stay here for the rest of our lives."

"Roger, you don't know how tired I am of King's Weltham!

If you hadn't been here, I'd have left long ago. How soon do you think we can get away?"

He looked at her doubtfully with an expression of sudden deep concern on his face. "Are you sure you mean that, Emma? Because I did mean what I said."

She nodded seriously. "Oh yes, I mean it. And I want to see a lot of the world while we're at it. We could make a long, slow journey of it, couldn't we, not wait to do that till we retire, like the Bushells? It could be the kind of journey one always remembers. Then perhaps we could begin to forget a few of the things that have happened in the last few days."

"You'll never forget Guy."

"I don't want to. What I want to forget . . ."

"Yes?" he said as she paused.

"I'd like to forget some of the things that haven't happened yet," she said. "Some terrible things are going to happen still. They must. And I'd like to blot them out and know nothing about them."

"Then don't you want to know who murdered Guy?"

"Not specially."

"I do," he said, "because I want to be sure who didn't. I don't want to have to go on wondering which of my old friends was capable of murder. I want them cleared."

"You think you know who did it, don't you, Roger? That theory of yours . . ."

". . . is only a theory. Let's forget it. Let's think about that ring we're going to buy. I've got lots of money, saved from my illegal sale of all those barbiturates."

She laughed. "So you know the police half suspect you of it."

"Only I don't think they really do," he said. "I think Day's just stirring things up all round to see what comes out of the hell broth. Now what about lunch?"

There was a good cold table at the George and both of them helped themselves to a variety of salads from the long counter down one side of the room and afterwards they went to the small antique shop in the square, which always had a modest but carefully chosen display of jewellery in its window. There was nothing there of much value, but most of it was charming. As soon as the tray was brought in from the window Emma knew which ring she wanted. It was a single fire opal on a narrow gold band. But she tried on ring after ring in case Roger had set his heart on one of the others, only to discover that he would not offer an opinion of any kind until she had shown plainly which one she liked best.

The owner of the shop, a young man with a high, bald forehead and a fringe of fair hair that curled over the collar of his velvet jacket, told them that opals were going up in value and that they had chosen wisely, and he was about to pack the ring in a small, silk-lined box when Emma slid it onto her left hand and said that there was no need to pack it up. He was probably ten years younger than she was, but he smiled at them as if they were two very young people on whose happiness it moved him to set this seal and he accepted Roger's cheque without even asking him to show his banker's card.

Back at the Institute he and Emma separated, Roger going upstairs, past the closed door of Guy's room, to his laboratory, and Emma along the passage to hers. But she stayed there for only a few minutes. Emotions that were both far more tumultuous and far more confusing than she had been prepared for had taken possession of her. She had not thought that marriage as such would mean much to her. She and Roger would go to a registrar who would say a few formal words, they would sign their names on a form, then they would go back to just where they had been before. Yet it turned out that it was not as simple as that. The truth was that an event of great importance had just happened to her—the decision not only to commit herself to marriage, but also for her and Roger to leave King's Weltham together—and she felt an intense urge to talk to someone about it.

Once she would have gone straight to Guy, who would have wished her joy, though with a sardonic look of reservation in his small grey eyes, which would have brought her down to earth, a place where on the whole she felt more at ease than she did floating among strangely coloured clouds, clouds as iridescent, as shot with sparks, as the fire opal on her finger. But there was no Guy in whom to confide, so she strolled along the passage to Ernest's office. Her cheeks were brighter than usual, but she kept both hands dug deep into her pockets, so that the ring did not show.

What she might have said if she had found Ernest quietly working she was never to know, for what she found was Ernest crouched over his desk with his face hidden in his arms and his thin shoulders shaken by sobs.

He heard her at the door and looked up. Tears were streaming down his face. For a moment he stared at her blindly, then he fished a handkerchief out of his pocket and mopped his eyes.

"I'm sorry about this," he mumbled.

"What is it, Ernest?" she asked. "What's happened?"

"An extraordinary thing. Utterly extraordinary." He blew his nose violently, gave another rub to his eyes, then returned the handkerchief to his pocket. "It bowled me over. Childish of me. I shouldn't have given way like this. But I've been under a great strain, that's why, I expect. Please don't tell anyone you saw it, Emma."

"Of course not, Ernest, but can't you tell me what the trouble is?" she asked.

"It isn't trouble, it's the opposite. I can still only half believe it." His reddened eyes swam again with tears. He brushed them away with his wrist. "Come in and shut the door. I don't want anyone else to catch me like this."

"Is it about your wife?" she asked, shutting the door, then taking the chair that faced him across the desk.

"Well, yes, in a way," he said. "Yes, of course, that's the whole thing. It's amazing. I've been going nearly out of my mind with worry, and now this happens. . . . I couldn't help it, I just broke down."

"Have you good news of her then? Is she better?"

He gave a quick shake of his head. "No, not that. You know, I've faced it, Emma, even if I've never said so, she's never going to be any better, not unless they come up with some new wonder drug that affects her condition, and I don't deceive myself that that's likely to happen in our lifetime. No, it's Guy—what he's done. He always told me I wasn't to tell anyone about it, but now he's dead I don't see that he could mind me telling you, of all people. I've just heard from his solicitors, Hubbard and Hubbard—no, I'm beginning at the wrong end of the story. Oh, God, I wish I had a drink. You haven't anything in your lab, have you?"

"Nothing but absolute alcohol."

He gave a watery smile. "Well, I expect I'm really better off without it. I don't want to get too maudlin. You see, Emma, the thing Guy didn't want me to tell anyone was that, ever since my wife went to Manstead House, he paid the fees. It started when I told him I was going to give up my job so that I could stay at home and look after her. I simply couldn't bear the thought of putting her into one of those great places on the National Health, where she'd be in a huge ward and no one, however good they were with her—and I know some of the doctors and nurses are wonderful—would ever have known that she had once been a real person whom one could love with all one's heart. So I decided to keep her at home and see what sort of disability pension I could get for her and do some sort of free-lance work to try to bring in a little extra money. But when I told Guy what I was going to do he simply wouldn't hear of it. He said I was going to need my job more than ever to keep myself sane, and that was true, of course, and that the thing to do was to find a good nursing home and that he'd pay the fees. At first I didn't believe he could mean it. I know he'd plenty of money, but how many rich people would think of doing a thing like that? And then when I began to realize he really did mean it, I told him I couldn't possibly accept charity like that and he told me not to be a fool. You know his way, snappish and overbearing, so that I almost got angry with him. But what a man he was, Emma! I've never known anyone like him."

With a tightness in her throat, Emma remembered how she and Roger had discussed the possibility that Ernest had eked out his salary by selling barbiturates. They had never thought of Guy as his source of support. For a moment she could not speak.

Ernest went on, "He even found Manstead House for me and arranged everything, because I wasn't capable of doing anything much at the time. And he made me keep on working and was often particularly hard on me, I think on purpose, and it was the saving of me." He leant back in his chair, giving a deep sigh. "It feels good to tell you this. I know a lot of people didn't like him. He'd a knack of making enemies. But sometimes when I've heard people like Bill Carver abusing him, I've thought, 'If you only knew the kind of man he really is!' But it was part of the deal that I wasn't to say anything about it, and I never did. And then—then he died . . ."

"And you thought the money was going to stop," Emma said. "That's why you've been so desperate, saying you didn't know what to do. But Guy's solicitors have told you it's going on. It's when you heard that that you broke down, isn't it?"

He drew a deep breath, let it out slowly, then nodded solemnly.

"I believe he's left most of his money divided among some nieces and nephews," he said. "But he made two special provisions in his will. One's to keep Dorothy for the rest of her life and one is to go on paying the fees at Manstead House for as long as my wife has to stay there. Isn't it extraordinary that he should have thought of that? But he was always very businesslike about his private affairs, just as he was about the affairs of the Institute. He liked to give you the impression of being casual and indifferent about practical things, leaving all that sort of thing to me, but actually he always knew everything that was going on and took all the important decisions himself. I suppose it's because of something he knew that he was murdered, for instance, who's been taking those barbiturates. Stan Rankin told me Guy said straight off he knew who it was and that he'd deal with it. And that could have been why he was killed."

"I wonder," Emma said. "Guy had two sides to his nature, you know. He could be very cruel if he didn't happen to like you, and I think he sometimes enjoyed being like that."

"But he was such a *good* man, Emma."

"To you and to me. But to some people he could be extraordinarily destructive."

The door opened. Bill Carver came in.

"Well, have you solved the mystery between you yet?" he asked. "It's the most popular parlour game in the Institute at the moment. 'Who killed Cock Robin?' Everyone's playing it. Unfortunately the police think they know who it was and there's shortly going to be an arrest. I thought you might be interested and that I'd come and break it to you gently."

There was nothing gentle about his manner. His voice was harsh and under the mockery of his words there was something rough, almost brutal. For an instant Emma felt sure that Bill had come to tell her and Ernest that the police were about to arrest Roger, whom Superintendent Day seemed to have favoured as a suspect from the start, and that Bill was enjoying being the one to tell her of it.

But she was doing him a wrong. Standing in the doorway

with his legs apart and his head held high, he thumped himself on the chest.

"Meet your murderer!" he cried dramatically. "They'll come to get me in a few minutes. I'd a motive—I hated Lampard's guts and never made a secret of it. I'd a weapon—I'd razors by the dozen. And I'd an opportunity. Does that surprise you? Well, it's true. That damned girl Maureen has told the police that she saw me go up the stairs to Lampard's office around twenty minutes to four, a few minutes before Hawse got back from his tea, and the fact is I did. So I think I may as well give myself up. I've no possible defence, have I?"

"Come in and sit down," Emma said.

Lurching into the room, Bill slumped onto a chair. It gave Emma a shock to realize that behind his sarcasm and his defiance he was frightened. There was an abnormal glitter in his eyes, which had lost their usual directness and become evasive and somehow crafty. Emma wondered how much truth there was in what he had just said.

"You went up to see Guy in the afternoon?" she said.

"Yes, and Maureen saw me." There were beads of sweat on Bill's forehead. "You know, I thought that girl liked me. Perhaps even something more than that. I'd a devil of a time when she first came here getting it over to her that I was a faithful husband. Trouble too persuading my wife she'd no reason to be jealous. I've no time for that sort of thing. Is that what's behind it, d'you think? Has she never forgiven me—Maureen, I mean? Is that why she went to the police with this story of hers?"

"I don't quite understand," Emma said. "The story's true, is it?"

"It's true that I went up to see Lampard, yes. And I knew Maureen had seen me. She came out of the common room as I was going up the stairs and she stood there watching me. When I came down I went straight to my lab and was sick in the sink. But she didn't say anything about seeing me to the police yesterday, so I thought I'd nothing to worry about. Then today, for some reason, she told them the whole thing. She's just been along to tell me about it, warning me, so to speak, that they'll be coming for me. She cried, said she was sorry, said they'd frightened her, sat there, the bloody bitch, wanting me to comfort her. She seemed to think a few tears would wipe out the damage she'd done. I could have strangled her."

"But if the story's true, perhaps she couldn't help herself," Emma said. "They may have found out something and put more pressure on her than she could stand."

"Then why didn't she tell them the truth straight away?" Bill demanded. "Then at least I'd have known where I was and wouldn't have told them the yarn I did about going straight to the common room from my lab. It might have taken some explaining, but it would have looked better than things do now."

Ernest was looking at him with a troubled frown. "You say you were sick in your sink," he said. "You mean Guy was dead already when you went in to see him."

"Of course he was," Bill said in a tone of extreme exasperation, "sitting there with a great slit in his throat and blood all over him. I've never been able to stand the sight of blood, I'm too damned squeamish. If I ever murdered anyone, I can tell you, it wouldn't be by cutting his throat. I'd slip some poison in his drink or some such thing. Actually I nearly passed out on the spot, but I managed to get back to my lab and didn't throw up till I got there."

"But why did you go to see Guy?" Emma asked. "Was he expecting you?"

"No, I suddenly made up my mind I'd make him see me. I thought I'd put it to him straight, would he support me if I gave his name as a reference when I applied for another job. I told you I'd been worrying about that. And there's a job going in Bristol I've been thinking I might apply for, but I knew he could ruin my chances of getting it if he was in one of his bloody-minded moods. So I decided I'd ask him straight out what he'd say if I gave his name. If he just laughed at me and told me I hadn't a chance of the job I'd have known I couldn't count on him, but if he'd told me to go ahead I'd have been fairly sure he wouldn't let me down. So I went off to see him before I could change my mind about trying it, and there he was, sitting at his desk, all blood. . . ." Bill clapped a hand over his mouth as if there were an imminent danger that he might be sick again.

"You know, Bill, you must only just have missed seeing the murderer," Ernest said.

Bill gave a wild look round the room, as if he half expected to see the murderer there, crouching in one of the corners.

"Did you see anyone in the hall besides Maureen?" Emma asked.

"No," he said.

"And you're sure you saw her come out of the common room. She wasn't just standing there as you went up?"

"No, I saw her come out of the door. If you're thinking of her as the murderess and that she'd just killed Lampard before she came downstairs, it won't wash, because the last thing she'd have done then would have been to come out of the room where there were lots of people to say she'd been there all the time."

"What I don't understand, Bill," Ernest said, "is why you didn't raise the alarm at once when you found Guy dead. It would have been the normal thing to do. You've got to admit that acting as you did looks horribly like a guilty conscience."

"Don't I know it!" Bill exclaimed. "But put yourself in my place. Everyone knew I detested Lampard, didn't they? Ever since I got here he never missed a chance of getting under my skin. Any time he could manage to humiliate me, he did. Look at the way he broke the news of Partlett's appointment in Bushell's place. He'd practically promised me Bushell's job when I first came here, and I'd been fool enough to believe him and to talk about it. So don't tell me the way he told us about Partlett wasn't deliberate. He wanted to make me look a fool. And the fact is, I went up to his room in a pretty murderous state of mind. If he'd jeered at me, which I was half expecting, I don't know what I might have done. So when I saw that someone had done it for me, and in that ghastly way, I was simply panic-stricken. I lost my head. I realized I was the perfect suspect. All I could think of was that I'd got to get away and hope no one would ever find out I'd been up there. I clean forgot about that bloody girl Maureen till later."

"I wonder why she came out of the common room then," Emma said thoughtfully. "She was in it when I got there. Did she tell you why she did when she came and cried on your shoulder?"

"I didn't ask her. I didn't think of it. Why?"

"It's something I'd rather like to know."

"Something I'd like to know, Bill," Ernest said, "is whether by any chance you're the person who changed the clocks. It seems to have been done to incriminate Partlett, and I know you hate Partlett almost as much as you hated Guy. If only you knew the sort of man he really was!"

"I knew all right." There was a bitter rasp in Bill's voice. "He was a first-class swine. And Partlett's the same, or worse. But I didn't change the clocks, though I don't expect you to believe me. I don't expect you to believe most of what I've been telling you." He stood up and went towards the door, moving as uncertainly as if he were drunk. "So the police aren't going to believe me either, are they? That girl's done for me, tied me up in pink ribbon and handed me to them in a gift-wrapped package. Well, see you at the trial. Enjoy the show, won't you?"

He started to laugh hysterically as he walked blunderingly out of the room.

Ernest gave a puzzled shake of his head. "Now who would ever have expected Bill to go to pieces like that?" he said. "I always thought of him as a rather tough character."

"Do you think he's a murderer?" Emma asked.

He met her eyes uneasily, fumbled for his handkerchief, blew his nose again and finally said, "The pity of it, Emma, that he should have felt about Guy as he did. Why couldn't he see under the surface to the real man?"

"The complicated thing is that I think the Guy he knew was as real as the one that you and I did," Emma said. "I think one's got to understand that if one wants to understand his murder." She stood up. "But I'm glad about his will, Ernest. You can stop worrying about your wife. I'm very glad Guy thought of it. Now I want a talk with Maureen. I've certain ideas about that young woman."

"Do you think she could have changed the clocks?" Ernest asked.

"I don't think so. I believe she went back into the common room with the rest of us. I remember she offered Mrs. Fielding some tea."

"Then do you think Bill changed them, whatever he says?"

"He does seem the likeliest person at present." But Emma was not thinking about the clocks. Another thought had come into her mind which seemed to her far more important. She left Ernest's office and went in search of Maureen.

Teatime had come round again and, as she expected, she found Maureen in the common room. There were not many people there that afternoon and those who had come were subdued and more silent than usual. Maureen was sitting alone at one of the tables with her back to the room, as if she did not want to talk to anyone. When Emma spoke to her she started, quickly drank what was left of her tea and got to her feet, saying that she must go back to her office as there was a great deal of work for her to get through. Her face had a pallid, empty look and reddened eyelids.

"The work can wait for a little," Emma said. "Come along to my lab, Maureen. I want to talk to you."

"But really I've piles of letters to do, Dr. Ritchie," Maureen protested. "I ought to get on with them. Dr. Challoner wants them done."

"Never mind about them for the moment," Emma said. "Come along with me. I don't want to talk here. I think it should be private."

That seemed to make Maureen still more apprehensive.

"Well, for a few minutes," she said uneasily, and followed Emma from the room.

In her laboratory Emma went to her usual chair at her desk and gestured to Maureen to sit on one of the stools, but the girl went to the window and stood there with her back to the room, looking massive yet vulnerable, as if her fine young body were wilting under the stress of the last two days. Emma realized that she had gone to the window on purpose to prevent Emma seeing her face and suddenly spoke to her sharply. "Look at me, Maureen."

The girl did not turn.

"I suppose you've been talking to Dr. Carver," she said.

"Yes," Emma answered.

"I didn't want to say anything about having seen him," Maureen said. "I'm sure he had nothing to do with the murder. But I couldn't help it."

"Why could you help it yesterday but not today?"

"I didn't understand things yesterday."

"What's made you understand them today?"

"Nothing. Nothing special. I did some thinking, that's all. I thought it would be best to tell the truth. I didn't think it would get Dr. Carver into trouble."

"It may get him arrested."

"But it was only the truth. At a time like this one's got to tell the truth, hasn't one?"

"If the police can put enough pressure on one to make one do it," Emma said.

Maureen turned round slowly, eyeing her warily. "I don't know what you mean."

"Well, let's start at the beginning." Emma wondered why she had never noticed before how much cunning there was in the girl's face. "You came out of the common room and you saw Dr. Carver going up the stairs to Dr. Lampard's office. Why did you come out?"

"I was going up to Dr. Lampard's office myself. He'd told me to. But just as I came out into the hall I saw Dr. Carver going up the stairs, so I waited and after a moment I saw him come down again and I wondered what could have happened, because he was looking terrible, and I noticed there was a great stain on the sleeve of his lab coat. I didn't really think about the stain at the time. It was red, but I thought it was some chemical or something. I never thought of it being blood. I mean, how could he get blood on himself in Dr. Lampard's office? So I forgot about it and it wasn't till this morning that I suddenly remembered it and thought of what it could mean and that really I ought to tell the police about it. I know it was stupid of me not to do it yesterday, but I'm afraid I think very slowly and I didn't want to get him into trouble."

"Why didn't you go up to Dr. Lampard's office, if he was expecting you, once you'd seen Dr. Carver come down?"

"Someone called to me from inside the room—wanted to talk to me about something or other, I forget what."

"Who was it?"

"I forget."

"Oh, Maureen, what's the point of lying?" Emma said. "Why try to keep from me what the police know already?"

A flush came into the girl's cheeks. "I don't see what right you've got to be asking me all these questions."

"No right at all. But why don't you simply admit you came out of the common room to meet Mrs. Fielding?"

"I didn't. It isn't true."

"It is, I think."

"What makes you say that?" There was a sulky look of helplessness on Maureen's face.

"Something Mr. Day said," Emma answered. "I felt at the time he'd said something important, though I didn't realize what it was. He said we couldn't be sure Mrs. Fielding was going up the stairs to Dr. Lampard's room, she might just as well have been going to Dr. Challoner's and only stopped where she did and started screaming because Dr. Lampard's door was open and she saw him in the room. But of course she could just as well have been going to your room and the fact that you left the common room and waited in the hall makes it look as if you were expecting her. Weren't you just going up to your room to wait for her when you saw Dr. Carver go up, and the way he came dashing out immediately, looking as strange as he did, scared you into deciding to wait till you were sure he was out of the way? You must have given Mrs. Fielding instructions where to find your room. You knew she could go straight to it without asking Arthur the way. And later, of course, when I'd left you and her together in here, you showed her the way out. I ought to have thought of that sooner. That side entrance isn't easy to find if you don't know your way about the building." She looked at Maureen's big, healthy body and added curiously, "D'you use the barbiturates yourself? You don't look like my idea of an addict."

Maureen gave a shrug of surrender. "No, I tried them once, but they only made me dopey." She sat down on one of the stools. "Who told you I'd taken them?"

"I just worked it out from the odd bits of information that came my way," Emma said. "Mostly your being in the hall when Dr. Carver went upstairs and the way that Mrs. Fielding disappeared when I'd left her in your charge. Guy knew it was you, didn't he?"

"Yes, I came here one Sunday, when I thought there wouldn't

be anyone about, and he saw me and didn't know what I was doing there, but when Stan Rankin told him the barbiturates were disappearing he guessed straight away. I began by denying it, but that didn't go down with him, so I just gave in and admitted it."

"Did he give you the sack?"

"No, he didn't." Maureen sounded as if there were something about this that still surprised her. "He just told me not to be a fool and to stop doing it before I got into real trouble. But of course I had to tell Mum I couldn't go on sending her the stuff and she came straight down here to persuade me to try to go on getting it for her. She wouldn't understand why I simply couldn't do it any more."

"Your mum!" Emma exclaimed. "Mrs. Fielding's your mother!"

"Her name isn't Fielding, it's Kirby, of course—yes, she's my mother. Fielding was her maiden name and she used it when you asked her who she was because it was the first one that came into her head. She's been on the stuff for ages. Of course I know it's bad for her, but she's even worse when she doesn't have it and her doctor won't prescribe it any more. And a chemist friend who used to sell it to her at a terrible price got into trouble with the police for pushing drugs, so she was in a pretty bad way."

"How did the police find out about it?" Emma asked.

"The same way you did, wondering why I'd gone out into the hall and waited there."

"But how did they know you'd done that? I heard it from Dr. Carver, but he hadn't told them about it."

"Someone in the common room told them he'd seen me go out and come in again a minute or two later, and they guessed it was to meet my mother, though of course they didn't know she was my mother. And then there was the way I'd helped her out of the building. And they kept on and on at me about it this morning till I admitted it and told them about seeing Dr. Carver to stop them bullying me."

"Why did your mother make up that crazy story about having been Dr. Lampard's mistress?"

"I think it was the only thing she could think of to explain why she was there. She wanted to keep me out of it, you see. She didn't want to let on she'd come here to see me in case it got me into trouble because of the drugs."

"And will it?"

"I don't know. When I talked to the police this morning they said they might not have to tell anyone about the drugs because they didn't think they had direct connection with the murder, but I don't know if they meant it. But just hoping that they did, I didn't want to tell you about it, because I'd like to keep my job here. Only now you know all about it, of course, I'll have to leave."

"Well, I think I understand why you like living with your grandmother in Crandwich better than with your parents in London," Emma said.

"I do," Maureen agreed. "But I know I'll have to go back to London now. I'll be sorry to go. I've liked it here." She stood up once more. "Is that all?"

Emma nodded. Briefly she wondered as the girl went out if it would be possible to give her a second chance, but that would be up to the new director, whoever he was. If Maureen did not resign of her own accord, he would have to be told the whole story, even if the police did not bring it into the open.

Maureen herself seemed to have no sense that she had done anything wrong. It was inconvenient to have been found out, but that was all. It was that attitude of hers, Emma thought, that gave her the air of vulnerable innocence that always made one feel sorry for her. Emma felt sorry for her now. She felt sorry for her because she had a mother who was a drug addict, because she was going to lose her job and most of all because she was stupid, a misfortune about which very little could be done.

It was beginning to grow dark in the room and Emma got up

to switch on the light, but as the overhead strip lights flickered on she thought that she might as well go home. There was nothing that she could do here and if Roger should come looking for her he would know where she had gone. She had just put on her coat and turned to the door when it opened and Roger came in.

"They've arrested Bill," he said baldly.

It seemed to surprise him that she showed no surprise.

"He was expecting it, you know," she said. "Maureen told them she'd seen him go up to Guy's room and come out again with blood on his sleeve."

"Yes, and they've found a witness who saw him stuffing his lab coat into the incinerator. And lots of people have told them the sort of things he used to say about Guy."

"But do you mean they've actually charged him with murder already?"

"Oh, I don't suppose so. But they've taken him to the police station to make a statement." He stood in the middle of the room, blinking as if he found the light suddenly too bright. "Emma, I don't think he did it."

"Why not?"

"Because I think I know who did."

"Ah, that theory of yours," she said.

"Yes, and I don't know what to do about it."

"Why not tell the police?"

"In case of being wrong after all. I've next to no evidence and I don't want to make things worse than they are already."

She unbuttoned her coat and sat down in her chair, ready to listen. It occurred to her that she had seldom seen him so inwardly unsure of himself. She was used to his outward show of diffidence but knew that behind it there was a strong core of certainty.

"Who is it?" she asked.

"Well, who really had cause to hate Guy? Whom had he really damaged? Whom was he doing his best to destroy?"

She hesitated, then answered questioningly, "Sam Partlett?"

He nodded. "Yes, Sam Partlett. He's a violent man, but he hates and fears his own violence. But Guy loved it. I think he was a violent man himself, and suppressing it, as he knew he'd got to if he wanted to make a career for himself, probably explains the contradictions in his nature. And probably it explains why he couldn't have any deep relationship with a woman. He was dead scared of what he'd have liked to do to her. But he could express all that through Sam. He knew how to work Sam up so that he'd lose all control of himself, smash up pubs and beat up his wife. But Sam thought he'd got over all that sort of thing. He'd been away from Guy for a fair time. He thought he'd be able to resist his tempting. But Faust couldn't resist Mephistopheles, could he, even when he knew it meant taking the way of damnation? And Sam was never able to resist Guy. He loved him too much."

"But, Roger, Sam couldn't have done it," Emma said. "He's got a perfect alibi. I'm the one person who knows for certain he has."

"There's got to be something wrong with that alibi."

"But there isn't, there really isn't."

He looked up at the clock on the wall. "How sure are you that that clock was right when you got back from the hairdresser? How sure are you that it hadn't been tampered with already?"

"Quite sure. I remember looking at it when I got in. It was twenty minutes past three. If it had already been put back ten minutes, the real time would have been half past three, which would have meant that I'd crawled back from Crandwich like a snail, which I didn't."

"Then Sam came in a few minutes later?"

"Yes, about twenty-five past three."

"But you realize that, if the clock was already wrong, the time he really came in was twenty-five minutes to four, which would have given him just time to do the murder without Arthur seeing him go in and out of Guy's room."

"But the clock wasn't wrong, Roger, it really wasn't. It was changed, with the other clocks, after the murder, and not by Sam, because he'd no need to change it. He knew I could give him an alibi. I think whoever changed it wanted us to think it had been changed earlier, which would have destroyed Sam's alibi. They couldn't have known I'd be so sure the clock was right when I got in."

Roger frowned at the clock. "I still think there has to be something wrong with that alibi. . . . Are you going home now?"

"Yes."

"I'll come as soon as I can."

She held out a hand to him, so that the light caught the glow of the opal on it; he took the hand, drew her to her feet and kissed her, then went out.

Emma buttoned up her coat again, took the car keys out of her handbag and went to her car.

The exhilaration of the afternoon, when she and Roger had been happy together for a little while, had left her. She thought of Bill, of his family, of the tragedy hanging over them, and tried to decide if she believed in his guilt. She wondered also if the superintendent believed in it or if he was playing some cunning game, the object of which she failed to understand. She was convinced that, for all the friendliness of his manner, he was a devious man who would act only with a high degree of wariness, not incautiously or in the least impulsively. But thinking along those lines, as she drove through the November dusk, got her nowhere. She turned in at her gate and was going to drive straight into the garage when just in time she realized that its doors were shut.

This was unusual. It was her habit and the Partletts' to leave the doors open until both their cars were in the garage. Getting out of her car, she went to the doors to push them open. As she did so the headlights of her car lit up what was inside.

Sam Partlett's body was hanging by what looked like a length of clothesline from one of the steel struts that supported the roof. His feet dangled a yard from the floor. When, only half aware of what she was doing, Emma rushed towards him and tried to lift him, to take his weight off that terrible cord, she could feel that there was still some warmth in his body, but she knew that she was not in time, as Guy had once been before her, to bring him back to life.

CHAPTER 9

Even if she had been in time, she would not have been able to cut him down by herself. She stood there helplessly for a moment, then went running to the steps that led down to the Hawses' flat. She did not know whether Arthur would be home yet, but if he was he could help her. Useless as it might be, she felt that it was impossible to leave that limp body dangling in space. She rang the bell imperatively.

Arthur himself opened the door.

"Please come with me, Arthur," she said. "At once. To the garage. No, don't bother about your coat. Just come. Please."

What he saw in her face made him hurry. They went out together along the pathway to the garage.

When he reached it he stood still, staring, but except for the startled lifting of his eyebrows he looked stolid and unmoved. Emma was filled with ferocious impatience.

"Quick, help me get him down," she said. "You've a stepladder, haven't you?"

He shook his head. "You can't do him any good and you didn't ought to touch him, Miss Ritchie. The police won't want you to do that."

"But perhaps we can still save him." She did not believe it, but she had to say it. "We can't leave him like that."

"Best thing to do." He looked round the garage. "You can see how he did it. Climbed on the bonnet of his car to take the jump. Not the way I'd choose if I wanted to kill myself, but they say he tried it once before. Everyone to his taste." He took a step forward, switching on the light in the garage. "Look, here's something."

Tucked under one of the windscreen wipers of the Partletts' car was an envelope. Pulling it out, he said, "It's addressed to you."

He handed it to her. She saw her name, "Emma," scrawled across it. As she took it and tucked it into a pocket she became aware that she had left her motor running. Switching it off, she turned to the house.

"Then wait here till I get a doctor," she said.

"Too late for that. Get the police."

"But if there's the slightest chance there's some life in him . . ."

"There isn't. I can tell."

Emma knew that he was right but felt appalled by her impotence. There ought always to be something that one could try to bring life back even to the certainly dead. It seemed a duty. That there was nothing made her angry, and the anger turned against Arthur for his common-sense obstructiveness.

"Well, stay here," she ordered, "while I telephone."

She went into her flat, sat down at the telephone and dialled the doctor, then the police station, and then tried to telephone Roger, but the switchboard girls at the Institute had gone home and she could not get through to anyone.

It was only after that that she began to think of Judith. She would have to go upstairs to tell her what had happened. But before doing that, she took the envelope out of her pocket and opened it.

Sam Partlett had had a jagged, untidy writing which she found difficult to read. Written with a ballpoint, it sprawled over a sheet of typing paper.

Dear Emma,
    I'm sorry about this, I know you'll be the one to find me

and that'll upset you. But I can't go on any longer. I don't deserve to live. I'm doing another experiment with death and I hope this time I'll find something out. I wish Guy hadn't saved my life the last time I tried it. It would have spared Judith a lot of unhappiness. She'd have married someone else and had a decent life. She'll be better off without me now. This will be a shock to her, but she'll get over it and probably really be glad of it. And the fact is, I knew I'd have to do it when I heard they'd arrested Carver. I've done some terrible things, like killing Guy in a sort of frenzy, but I can't go on in cold blood. Carver's got a wife and kids and I can't let all their lives be ruined. Mine's ruined anyway. I killed Guy, I suppose you could say, out of revenge for the way he turned me into a monster. Look at the things I've done to Judith. Not that they weren't my own fault, I know they were, but Guy loved the streak of madness in me. It gave him a thrill to see what I'd do. So in the end I turned against him. I did kill him, you know. You were wrong about that alibi. I changed the clock in your room before you got back from Crandwich. I don't know why you've been so certain I didn't. It wasn't twenty-five past three when I came to see you, it was twenty-five to four, and I'd just been up to Guy's room, just after Hawse had gone off to have his tea, taken only a minute to kill Guy, because of course he was taken completely by surprise, got blood on my hands, but not on my clothes, because I'd turned my sleeves back, went back to my lab and washed, then went in to see you. The reason I changed the other clocks when I changed yours was that I didn't know when you'd be coming back that afternoon. You might not have come back at all. In that case I'd have gone in to chat to Carver, so that he'd be the one to give me an alibi. I changed the clocks in the lunch hour, when he'd gone home. But Nixey was in his room, eating sandwiches there,

as I suppose he hasn't got a home to go to, so I couldn't get
into his room, but I changed the clock in his secretary's
office and hoped that would help to muddle things up, so
that no one could be sure when anything happened. When
I came out of Guy's room there was no one in the hall, because the main crowd hadn't started coming down for tea
yet from upstairs, and I bolted to my lab and then went in
to see you and thought I'd pulled it off. But I didn't think
of anyone else being arrested for what I'd done. Well, I
think that's all. You can give this to that policeman. I'm
only writing to you because I know you'll be the one to find
me and, as I said, I'm sorry about that. You've been very
good to Judith and me.

Sam

The scrawl became steadily more illegible as the letter progressed, with the lines sloping more and more crookedly across
the paper. Emma read it twice, then folded it and put it
back in its envelope. She put it down beside the telephone and
at that moment heard the click of the latch of her front door and
knew that it was Roger coming in. He must already have been
on his way to the village when she tried to telephone him at the
Institute.

She saw from his face that he had already seen into the garage. She handed him Sam's letter without speaking. Like her,
he read it twice, then folded it and returned it to its envelope.

"So after all you were wrong about his alibi," he said.

"Yes," she answered.

"I knew there had to be something wrong with it," he said.

She nodded.

He seemed a little surprised that she did not argue.

"Perhaps the clock in your hairdresser's was slow," he said.
"Perhaps you left there later than you thought, so the time you
took to get back to King's Weltham seemed normal."

"Yes."

"That's how it must have been."

"Yes." She stood up wearily. "Someone's got to go up to Judith. Will you wait for the doctor and the police while I go?"

He put an arm round her, holding her tightly for a moment. "Don't take this too hard, Emma. You did everything for those two that you possibly could."

"Except see into the future," she answered. "I'll go now."

"Would you sooner I went?"

"No, I think it would be best if I—if I had a talk with her."

"D'you want to show her this?" He held the envelope out to her.

"Yes, I suppose I'd better. We can show it to the police afterwards."

She took the letter and, with a look on her face that seemed to puzzle Roger, went out of the front door of her flat and rang the bell beside the Partletts'.

She heard Judith coming slowly down the stairs. For once she was not in her dressing gown but in the slightly too tight green corduroy suit in which she had first arrived. It brought back to Emma her first impression of Judith, her shyness, her look of being oddly young and undeveloped for her age. In his way, Sam had had the same look. Emma wondered how many murderers had it and were murderers because at some time in their early youth, when they were still inarticulate and violent action of some sort, screaming, kicking, breaking things, was the only way in which they could express their feelings, they had got stuck and their growth ever after had been crooked and lopsided because of it.

Judith took her upstairs into the living room, which still had as few of the Partletts' personal belongings in it as when they had first arrived. The room was warmed by the central heating, but it felt cold to Emma, with the chill of profound, unforgiving unhappiness.

"I've got to tell you about Sam, Judith," she said. Neither of them had sat down but were facing one another in the middle of the room in a way that gave them the look of being antagonists, preparing to do battle. "I don't know how to tell you this, but I suppose the simplest way is best. He's dead. He hanged himself from one of the struts in the garage. I found him and I've telephoned for the doctor and the police. Roger and Arthur are down there with him now."

Judith did not stir. She looked woodenly at Emma.

"So he's done it at last," she said. "I always thought he would sooner or later." Her voice was expressionless.

"He left this for me," Emma said, and held out Sam's letter to Judith.

She took it and read it quickly. His handwriting appeared to present no problem to her. Nothing changed in her face as she read.

"So now you know," she said, handing it back to Emma.

"Yes, I know."

"I've known from the first, of course. He told me. But a wife doesn't have to give evidence against her husband."

"Or a husband against his wife. There isn't a word of truth in that letter, is there?"

Judith's large, dark eyes widened a little. "I don't understand."

"I shouldn't have to spell it out to you," Emma said. "My clock wasn't wrong when I got back from Crandwich. Sam didn't change the clocks in the lunch hour. He did it after the murder. He knew you'd done it and he also knew he'd a perfect alibi and if you were suspected he couldn't protect you. So he went round changing the clocks, hoping it would be thought he'd done it earlier, because if my clock was ten minutes slow when I got in, then he hadn't an alibi at all. And naturally, as I was sure my clock was right when I got in, we thought at first it had been changed by someone who wanted to incriminate him, as he was the only person it affected. What we didn't think of was that he'd done it to incriminate himself."

"You're only guessing," Judith said in the same lifeless tone as before.

"But you want to hear the rest of it, don't you, or you'd have gone straight down to the garage? The news of Sam's death doesn't seem to have moved you much."

"I told you, I've lived with the thought of it for a long time. And I suppose you could say that hanging himself was symbolic. Punishment, the thing he craved all along."

Her coldness filled Emma with repulsion. "I know what he's done to you," she said. "I've seen something of it. But in the end he did his best to protect you."

"That was only because of his feelings of guilt. He felt that he'd murdered Guy, even if his hand didn't hold the razor."

"And he knew that yours did and he'd driven you to it."

Judith gave a shrug and turned away. She sat down. "Go on. We've no witnesses. Even if I admit what you're saying, I can contradict it later."

Emma did not want to sit down. She did not want the feeling that this conversation could drift into a cosy chat. She remained standing where she was, still with the sense of an unnatural chill in the room, though she knew that in reality it was inside herself.

"It began as soon as you got here, didn't it?" she said. "Guy had his old effect on Sam, perhaps all the stronger because they'd seen so little of each other for a long time. It was a terrible mistake for the two of you to come here."

"You don't have to tell me that," Judith said. "But Sam and I had been getting along pretty well for a good while. He seemed fairly stable and I didn't think it was too much of a risk to come. And no one else was offering him a job. I was horribly wrong."

"As you found out almost at once. Guy took him to the White Hart and got him drunk and sat there enjoying the show when Sam tried to smash the place up. I saw it. That's what Guy was like. Then Sam came home and beat you up. And then that nearly happened again after my party. He went to see Guy to tell him he was leaving, but Guy got some drinks into him and persuaded him to change his mind and he came home and started getting violent again. Roger and I heard it. But then something suddenly stopped him. Everything went quiet."

"So far you've said nothing new," Judith said.

"Well, I think I know what stopped him—perhaps that's new. I think you'd found a razor in the pocket of the jacket he usually wore. He must have dropped it in there absent-mindedly when he was in the lab, then he changed into a suit to come to the party and left the jacket lying about somewhere and for some reason you moved it, perhaps to hang it up, and the razor fell out. Or perhaps it didn't happen just like that. Perhaps he took it out of his pocket himself and said something about having been a fool for having brought it home, and left it lying about. Anyway, you had it, and when you saw he was in one of his violent moods you flicked it open and threatened him with it. And that stopped him on the spot. But naturally next day he remembered it. When Guy was killed with a razor, he was sure at once you'd done it. Perhaps you'd even told him the evening before that you were going to."

"Perhaps I did. One says these things. They don't mean anything." But Judith gave a sudden little smile, as if she were enjoying a memory.

Emma went on. "I think you must have gone in and out of the Institute like a zombie, not caring who saw you. Perhaps that's the best state of mind to be in when one commits a crime. But actually if anyone had seen you go in, you needn't have gone ahead with it. You could simply have gone to see Guy to tell him he'd got to leave Sam alone, or some such thing. But no one saw you, and of course he had no fear of you, so it was easy for you to get behind him and kill him. Perhaps having been a nurse told you just where to slash. And when you'd done that and wanted to leave a few minutes later, I suppose you looked out of the door to see if the coast was clear and when it was you made a dash for it. Actually, if you'd stayed only another minute or two, Bill Carver would have walked in on you, but you had luck and got away in time. I don't know where you'd left the car, but as Sam usually walked to the Institute you'd got it, and you got away in it and were home in time to take Sam's telephone call when he told you not to worry, everything would be all right. Then you had a bath to get rid of the blood you must have got on yourself, and washed your hair and whatever you were wearing, and put on your dressing gown and came down to tell Roger and me about Sam's call, making out, when we told you about the murder, that Sam had been telling you not to be afraid he'd be suspected. But really you couldn't bear it any longer by yourself, not knowing what had happened at the Institute, and of course what Sam had really been trying to tell you was that you needn't worry about yourself, that he'd changed the clocks and would take the blame if he had to. But Ernest Nixey walked in when Sam was in the middle of the call and he broke it off. I wonder what you wanted then. Did you hope Sam would be suspected?"

"Would you blame me if I did?" Judith asked.

"Not very much," Emma answered. "I know what you've been through."

"You don't. No one could know. And that evil man, Guy Lampard, was behind it all. He deserved to die. I've no regrets."

"He wasn't all evil," Emma said. "Far from it. He could be generous and good."

"To me he was the personification of evil," Judith said. "You called me a zombie. That's what I've been for days, with no thought in my mind but how to destroy him before he destroyed

179

Sam and me. I was too slow about it and it didn't work and Sam's gone too and that can't be helped. I'm sorry about it, but perhaps it's the best way out for him. That letter of his is more than half true, you know. He did kill Guy, though he did it through me, and if Bill Carver had been arrested he'd have gone crazy with guilt. I wonder if the police guessed Sam had done it and arrested Bill to draw Sam into the open."

Emma thought that this was not unlikely. Superintendent Day might be capable of it.

"And you won't go crazy with guilt yourself?" she said.

"No, I'll have some real peace of mind for the first time for years—though that depends on you. What are you going to do about all this?"

"I'll give the police Sam's letter."

"And that's all?"

"I didn't say that. But as you pointed out, there aren't any witnesses to this conversation. You could deny everything you've said to me. All the same, if I were you . . ."

"Well?"

"I believe if you confessed, and I told the court everything I know about your life with Sam, and you got a psychiatrist to help you, you wouldn't get anything very terrible in the way of a sentence. And then you'd have real peace of mind."

Judith bent forward, resting her face on her hands, her dark hair falling forward over it.

After a moment she said, "I'll have to think about it. Taking my time isn't going to make much difference to Sam. You know, I only stayed with him because I thought it was the right thing to do, but perhaps I did him as much damage as Guy did. But you're going to tell all this to the police, aren't you?"

"To Roger, anyway. He wasn't surprised at Sam's confession. He said he was the person whom Guy had really damaged. But I thought of you. I thought you were the one who'd really suffered."

"Of course, Roger. Do you know how lucky you are to have Roger? If only I'd met someone like him, instead of Sam. Or was the violence always there in me, just as it was in him, wanting to come out? Was that why I loved him, just as Guy did?"

"I don't know much about that sort of thing," Emma said. "I feel more at home with quantities I can measure on a balance or in a spectrophotometer. I'm going down now. Hadn't you better come with me? That would only look normal."

"Tell the police to come and talk to me. Tell them I'm too shattered to come down."

A statement, Emma thought as she turned to the door, which might be far nearer the truth than Judith herself realized. That frozen self-control might splinter at any moment. And when that happened, Superintendent Day, like a kindly family doctor, with the steel inside him hardly showing, would no doubt pick up the pieces without needing any assistance from Emma.

She went quietly downstairs and let herself out of the door at the bottom. She had done all she could. She had warned Judith. She had advised her. She had even, up to a point, in her heart, forgiven her. And now all that she wanted was something of which she knew there was no possibility whatever, a quiet evening alone with Roger.

ABOUT THE AUTHOR

E. X. FERRARS lives in Scotland with her husband who is a professor at the University of Edinburgh. She is the author of many crime novels, including *The Pretty Pink Shroud*, *Blood Flies Upwards*, *The Cup and the Lip*, and *Drowned Rat*. When not concocting mysteries of her own, she enjoys traveling, or the mysteries of cooking and gardening—and reading other writers' mysteries.

The latest thrilling mystery
by the author of THE ROSARY MURDERS

MIND OVER MURDER

WILLIAM KIENZLE

Monsignor Thomas Thompson has vanished. All that remains are his abandoned luxury car, a spent .32 caliber bullet—and a list of the faithful with motives for murder, meticulously recorded in Monsignor's scandalous diary. Clearly it's a case for Father Bob Koesler—parish priest, Sunday golfer, mystery buff—who is obliged to breach a tenet of faith to bring the devil himself to confession.

"Even the most astute thriller fan will find the ending to this rousing, labyrinthine tale a mind-blowing surprise."

—*Publishers Weekly*

(#20666-4 • $2.95)

Read MIND OVER MURDER, on sale June 15, 1982, wherever Bantam paperbacks are sold or order directly from Bantam by including $1.00 for postage and handling and sending a check to Bantam Books, Dept. MO, 414 East Golf Road, Des Plaines, Illinois 60016. Allow 4-6 weeks for delivery. This offer expires 12/82.

AND DON'T MISS THE OTHER FATHER KOESLER MYSTERIES:

THE ROSARY MURDERS (#14930-X • $2.75)
DEATH WEARS A RED HAT (#14429-4 • $2.75)

WHODUNIT?

Bantam did! By bringing you these masterful tales of murder, suspense and mystery!

☐	20572	**THE WHITE PRIORY MURDERS** by Carter Dickson	$2.25
☐	20375	**DEATH IN FIVE BOXES** by Carter Dickson	$2.25
☐	20435	**SLEEPING MURDERS** by Agatha Christie	$2.75
☐	14981	**THE MYSTERIOUS AFFAIR** **AT STYLES** by Agatha Christie	$2.50
☐	20155	**THE SECRET ADVERSARY** by Agatha Christie	$2.50
☐	20776	**THE RELIGIOUS BODY** by Catherine Aird	$2.25
☐	20271	**THE STATELY HOME MURDER** by Catherine Aird	$2.25
☐	14797	**BEFORE MIDNIGHT** by Rex Stout	$2.25
☐	13783	**SOME LIE & SOME DIE** by Ruth Rendell	$1.95
☐	13039	**A SLEEPING LIFE** by Ruth Rendell	$1.95
☐	13948	**THE FINGERPRINT** by Patricia Wentworth	$1.95
☐	20038	**TOO MANY CLIENTS** by Rex Stout	$2.25
☐	14546	**CASE CLOSED** by June Thomson	$1.95
☐	14930	**THE ROSARY MURDERS** by William Kienzle	$2.75
☐	13784	**NO MORE DYING THEN** by Ruth Rendell	$1.95

Buy them at your local bookstore or use this handy coupon for ordering: